Prai:

All Roads Lead to Lawrence

"Every day, I teach my student athletes that playing college basketball is a metaphor for life. We teach accountability on the court, in the classroom, and in their social life. In *All Roads Lead to Lawrence*, Zeke's challenge is to use the lessons learned on the court to overcome obstacles and navigate his way in the real world."

JOE PASTERNACK
Men's Head Basketball Coach
UC Santa Barbara

"*All Roads Lead to Lawrence* is the fiction equivalent of a fast break and a slam dunk! Leener takes us on a fun and imaginative ride full of rich characters and fast pivots, and infuses it throughout with pure love of the game."

CLARK PETERSON
Film and Television Producer
Academy Award Winner for *Monster*

"I enjoyed the pacing and chapter breaks, which are perfectly segmented with regard to dramatic structure, and I feel the book could be easily adapted for a screenplay. The vivid descriptions of the settings, be they the gymnasium or Zeke's visitations with the 7th Dimension, lend themselves well to a wide range of visual effects. The universal themes of friendship, loyalty, brotherly love, and sportsmanship are perfectly suited to today's younger movie-going audience. Those poignant sentiments, coupled with state-of-the-art digital imagery and sound design, would make for a compelling film."

THEO GLUCK
Film Historian and Preservationist
Burbank, California

"The story of Zeke shares the conflict, tragedy, and development from teenager to young adulthood. The use of basketball and its history bridges the gap of generations and helps people to appreciate today's youth. *All Roads Lead to Lawrence* is a must read!"

HOWARD FISHER
Head Coach, Youth Men's Basketball Team for Team USA

"Not since I read Bernard Malamud's *The Natural* have I enjoyed the character development and irony of a story this much. There were elements that touched my own life—from Coach Kincaid's decisions, to having a Chip Spears in my corner, to a first girlfriend like Rebecca, to Lawrence's inspirational and relevant message."

GREG HERRICK
Head Women's Basketball Coach
College of the Canyons

"In this outstanding follow-up to his debut novel, Leener takes his characters on a moving and inspiring journey that explores friendship with humor and suspenseful twists. It is a magnificent achievement. Imaginative and powerful storytelling ... nothing but net!"

JAMES ENZO GENTILCORE
Vice-Chairman, Vidfilm International Digital

"Leener is writing for an untapped market—teenagers and soon-to-be teenagers who like basketball AND books, and he writes in a way that grabs their attention and takes them on a wild and unexpected ride."

MATTHEW LIEBERMAN
Author of *The Sugarmans* and currently writing
for TV's *Queen of the South*

"As a songwriter, I strive to use rhythm, dynamics, tone, texture, and form to create music that has emotional impact. In much the same way, propelled by a truly imaginative story and unforgettable characters, Craig Leener has succeeded brilliantly with his second novel."

STEVE WILLIAMS
Singer-Songwriter

"The author has scored the winning bucket with this intelligent and heartfelt analysis of friendship and redemption. Zeke and his buddies explore the many layers of loyalty, love, and loss as they shoot for answers that are found well beyond a metal basketball hoop."

DeMONT WALKER
Author of *The Lake of Illumination: Convergence*

"This book was exciting, funny, and kept me interested. I was surprised by the many twists, and other readers will be as well. *All Roads Lead to Lawrence* is perfect for any kid who likes basketball, science, and math."

SANTOS RODRIGUEZ
Avid reader and youth basketball player
Murrieta, California

"Passion, anguish, and victory—on and off the court—fuel this fascinating tale of Zeke, a community college student athlete with a whole lot going on in his life. There's no need to be a basketball fan to get a lot out of this book that grabs you by the jersey and doesn't let go until the final buzzer."

STEPHANIE BLUESTEIN, Ed.D.
Associate Professor of Journalism
California State University, Northridge

"Zeke confronts heartbreak and the ultimate questions of human existence, using the analogy of basketball to make sense of it all. The book has everything from extraterrestrials to consciousness beyond death and telepathic sea creatures, from teamwork and friendship to learning how to give a proper handshake. I was delighted to see Lawrence and his bubble-gum show up again, and his new friend Nathan."

SARAH HOPE GOSS
Licensed Marriage and Family Therapist

"This book was definitely one of the best books I have ever read. I thought this second book went along very well with the first. It picked up the story in a good part and also added a lot of new and exciting events. The ending was also great. I can't wait for the next book."

DREW WESCHLER
Avid reader and youth basketball player
Apex, North Carolina

"The author takes us on an exciting journey that enables us to stream into higher states of consciousness and understand what we are and all the probabilities that await us beyond the physicality of human life. It is a feel-great book that invites us to understand that death, as we know it, is non-existent. *All Roads Lead to Lawrence* is a magnificently well-written novel."

CHRISTIAN FIECH
Meditation Teacher

"A marvelous follow-up to its predecessor, *All Roads Lead to Lawrence* triangulates on the importance of maintaining your passions, developing true friendships, and growing from the obstacles and lessons life throws at you. Zeke's continued tale of adventure and personal redemption is beautifully set against a real-world backdrop that mixes brilliantly with the game of basketball, the imaginative wonders of theoretical physics, and the power of friendship—all of which gives readers another thrilling ride."

JESSE MUÑOZ
Director of Public Relations & Sports Information
College of the Canyons

"The story of Zeke Archer is a riveting tale of struggle and self-discovery. Every chapter of Zeke's journey in basketball and in life is engrossing, and I'm looking forward to his next adventure."

SAM HERTZOG
Avid reader and high school basketball player
Lawrence, Kansas

"Craig Leener offers readers a fascinating glimpse into the world of the 7th Dimension. Here's a hint: as junior college chess champion Nathan Freeman says in the book, it's a ballet of the mind."

VICKY SKANE
Children's Librarian (retired)
Moses Lake, Washington

ALL ROADS LEAD TO LAWRENCE

ALL ROADS LEAD TO LAWRENCE

CRAIG LEENER

To uncle Nat:

I've always appreciated
your love and support.

GREEN BUFFALO
PRESS

— Craig

To Dr. James Naismith

for his eternal gift of the game of

basketball to the world

And to Andrea

for making everything in my life possible

CONTENTS

CONTENTS

ALL ROADS LEAD TO LAWRENCE

1

Magical Things Could Happen

I had practiced *the play* on the rec center's basketball court a million times before.

Now, on a spring afternoon in Los Angeles, I was running it for real, in the biggest game of my life—the Southern California Regional Championship—on our home court, the gymnasium at Jefferson Community College.

My name is Zeke Archer, and that's where this strange tale begins.

My stories always begin with basketball. And it's through basketball that I measure my life and figure out the people who are in it. I am more confident on a basketball court than I am anywhere else on earth.

The game, which was taught to me years ago by my older brother, Wade, always reveals the truth.

Our team was on defense and trailing our crosstown rivals from Westside City College, 77–76, with ten seconds left to go, when the Westside coach called a timeout to draw up his team's final play. It was a good thing he did too—we were out of timeouts and running on fumes.

The crowd stirred and buzzed as our coach, Coach Kincaid, waved us over to the sideline. Our shooting guard, Curtis Short, playing on a sprained ankle, plopped down onto the bench, his face contorted in pain. Our seven-foot-two-inch center, Roland "Stretch" Puckett, cranked his lanky frame forward, hands on hips, gasping for oxygen.

Curtis and Stretch were my best friends. Curtis's devotion to basketball was exceeded only by his love of surfing. Stretch's desire for a career as a private investigator was eclipsed only by his fondness for food.

Our two forwards, Brock Decker and Jed Swagerty, weren't in much better shape. They were winded and drenched in sweat.

Coach Kincaid had a knack for calming us down when the pressure was mounting and the stakes were high. He set down his clipboard and glanced at the scoreboard.

"It's only one point, gentlemen, and ten seconds is an eternity," Coach Kincaid said. "Man-to-man defense. Go for the steal on the inbounds pass. If you don't get it, foul whoever catches the ball. We'll put him on the free-throw line and win it on the other end."

Sure thing, Coach. Simple enough. Do the near impossible in less time than it takes to lace up a pair of high-tops—and do it on an empty tank.

"Got it, Coach," I said. "C'mon, guys, let's go get us some hardware."

That's what my teammates expected me to say, because I was Jefferson's team captain and all-conference point guard. But beyond the mere words, I really believed we could pull it off. The hardware up for grabs was the So-Cal championship trophy.

The referee blew his whistle and handed the basketball to the Westside player who was taking it out of bounds. The kid slapped the ball with his hand, cuing his teammates to dart around the court in all directions in search of daylight. I turned my back on the guy I was guarding to make it seem as if I were going after a different player. Then I waited a beat, whirled around, and stepped into my opponent's path.

I intercepted the inbounds pass, setting into motion *the play*—a three-on-two fast break. Wade had once told me that if I ran a fast break to perfection, magical things could happen.

Wade was in the Marine Corps, in Afghanistan, serving our country in a war on the other side of the globe. I would have settled for the magical thing being Wade shouting encouragement and instructions from the bleachers. But he was a few weeks away from coming home to Los Angeles for good, so that wasn't an option. Instead, I would have to figure out how to win it without him.

The fast break is an offensive strategy in which the point guard takes the ball up court so swiftly that the defense doesn't have a chance to set up. My job in that moment was to maneuver the ball across half court and force the two out-numbered, back-pedaling defenders to commit to a defensive plan of action. Once they did, I would choose my best op-tion—pass to an open teammate for a layup, take the shot from the free-throw line, or dish off to a teammate trailing the play behind me for a mid-range jumper.

And I needed to decide by the time I got to the charity stripe fifteen feet from the basket. I had to make a split-sec-ond decision and live with the consequences.

I took off down court as Curtis speed-shuffled across the hardwood to my right. Stretch filled the lane on my left, gal-loping like a giraffe pursued by a starving lion. Fans rose to their feet as the two Westside defenders scrambled backward. *The play* we had practiced so many times before was unfold-ing right before my eyes.

Perfectly.

Then, when I pulled up at the free-throw line, it happened. My life, as they say, would never be the same.

2

That Put Me at the Crossroads

Everything went black.

At first, I thought someone had turned out the lights in the gym. I blinked a couple of times. The light leaked back in. I realized I was no longer standing on a basketball court.

I was crouched on my haunches on the bottom of a sandy crater beneath the scorching sun. The sound of Jefferson's pulsating crowd dissolved into a whir of truck engines. And I still had the ball.

What in the world was going on?

I eased up my head to look around. As I did, a wave of heat raked across my skin. The stink of diesel exhaust invaded my nostrils. I was standing up to my neck in a sandy pit in the middle of a barren, lifeless desert.

All at once, an intense flash of light blinded me. Then a thunderous explosion jolted the earth all around me. My ears stung from the shockwave of the blast. I heard faint screams off in the distance. Then everything went black again.

When I came to, I was standing at the foul line as if nothing had happened and no time had elapsed. For the life of me, I had no idea what had just gone down.

I gathered my wits instantly and sized up the play. Curtis and Stretch were covered—there was no way I could get the ball to either of them. I arched my body in preparation for a jump shot, but the player guarding Curtis reversed course and came right at me. Out of the corner of my eye, I caught a glimpse of Brock Decker behind me and to the left, wide open and motioning wildly for the ball just inside the three-point line.

That put me at the crossroads.

I only had two options left: take the shot with a defender in my grill or flip the ball over my shoulder to Brock for an uncontested eighteen-footer.

I chose to take the shot.

I launched a jumper from the free-throw line, straight as a salmon going upstream.

And a foot short.

The basketball grazed the bottom of the net as the final horn sounded. It landed on top of one of Stretch's size 18 shoes, propelling the ball to the other side of the court.

That's where a kid wearing weird clothing from a bygone era scooped up the ball with his foot. He caught it with both hands and drop-kicked it, rugby-style, toward the basket I had just whiffed at.

The ball ricocheted off the glass backboard and slammed through the hoop.

I looked back to where the kid was standing, but he had vanished into thin air.

3

There's No Shame in the Outcome

I turned back around and was met by two muscular meat hooks shoving me hard to the deck.

"Way to go, dweeb. I was wide open." It was Brock Decker. "I guess you wanted the glory all for yourself. Get up, Pencil Neck, so I can drop you again." My relationship with Brock could best be described as complex.

I sprung to my feet. Without thinking, I lunged at Brock. Curtis and Stretch blocked my path.

"That's enough, gentlemen!" Coach Kincaid said as he stormed over to us. I had never seen Coach so angry. "In case you fellas hadn't noticed, you're on the same team. Why don't you do something constructive, like congratulate your opponents."

"Sorry about that, Coach K," Curtis said.

We turned around to witness Westside City College fans high-fiving each other as the players dogpiled in celebration at center court. Brock muttered an obscenity and bolted in the opposite direction. Curtis and Stretch tried to bring me back to Earth.

"Dude's a cement-head, bro," Curtis said. "Let it go."

"Even though you air-balled the game winner, I liked your chances a little better than Brock's," Stretch said in a questionable attempt to offer reassurance.

The guys and I shook hands with the Westside players and walked to our bench to gather our gear. Coach Kincaid intercepted me.

"Did you make the right decision on that play?" Coach asked.

Coach was always asking the good ones. "I think so," I said without thinking. The truth was, I didn't know.

Coach Kincaid had a familiar look in his eyes, the gleam that always appeared just as he would get ready to go deep. "This game mirrors life in so many ways. It often comes down to sizing up your options and making the right decision. I have a sense that's what you did. There's no shame in the outcome."

By then, the outcome I was looking for was riding my bike home and escaping into a hot shower. I picked up my gym bag and took another look around for the teenager who had banked home the full-court dropkick.

4

It Had to Be a Mistake

"Looking for someone?"

It was my girlfriend, Rebecca Tuesday, who also happened to be Brock's stepsister, which added to the complexity of my relationship with Brock. I had gotten to know Rebecca the previous year, when we were both seniors at Ernest T. McDerney Continuation School.

But I had first met Rebecca years earlier at the rec center, one day when I was playing pickup basketball with Curtis and Stretch. Brock showed up with this girl named Becky, and he wanted us to let her play. We weren't big on the idea, but we reluctantly agreed. A couple of minutes into the game, I fractured Becky's nose with my elbow when I came down with a rebound. I didn't see her again until the day she walked into the cafeteria at McDerney Continuation at the beginning of senior year—and I didn't realize that Rebecca and Becky were the same person until weeks later.

McDerney was the place where Curtis and Stretch and I rode out our final high-school semester after we were expelled from Southland Central High because of a fight I started during the city finals. Brock, on the opposing team, took a cheap shot at Stretch by clotheslining him on a fast break as we were about to take the lead in the closing seconds. I lost my temper and took a swing at Brock, but I missed and slugged the referee instead. That cost us the game—and my full-ride basketball scholarship to the University of Kansas. I had been trying to put my life back together ever since.

A big part of all that was Rebecca. To put it bluntly, I was nuts about her. She was cute and smart, and she had a social conscience. But sometimes things got weird too, because she had a dark side that would surface from time to time. She would go silent and push me away, and I had no idea why. When that happened, I was totally lost. Because as confident as I was on a basketball court, I was anything but confident in most everything else—especially when it came to girls.

"That was a tough one," Rebecca said. "It looked like you had a lot on your mind when you tossed up that brick."

Stretch must have overheard our conversation, because he cruised over and appeared to be laying down some ground cover. "I think someone opened a door at the exact wrong moment, and Zeke shot the ball into the wind."

"Uh-huh." I could tell that Rebecca wasn't buying it.

I know this is going to sound lame, but I had taken the

shot because I didn't want Brock to have to live with the regret he would feel if he missed it and cost us the championship. As team captain, I thought that burden should be mine
and mine alone.

"You look like you could use a shoulder right now," Rebecca said.

"Next time. Right now, I need a long bike ride and a longer shower," I said without thinking. *What an idiot.* Rebecca
was trying to ease the hurt, and now *I* was pushing *her* away.

Before I could say anything more, a member of the press
corps accosted me.

"Zeke, what happened on that last play? It looked like you
hesitated."

That was Darla Davenport, a sports reporter for the *Jefferson
Journal*, the college's newspaper. I liked Darla as a classmate,
even though her timing in that moment was unwelcome. She was
passionate about sports journalism, and she was persistent.

I watched Rebecca head to the door of the gym and wished
I could catch up with her.

"I tried my best to put my team in a position to win," I
told Darla. "I was hoping for a better outcome, but it just
didn't happen."

How could I tell Darla that the real reason why I had
hesitated was that the hardwood floor had turned into a desert landscape on the most important play of my basketball
career to date.

I answered the rest of Darla's questions before making my
way out of the arena and pedaling for home. A half hour later,
I arrived at my apartment and carried my bike up the stairs. As

I neared the top of the staircase, I was met there by two men in military uniforms. I moved to one side to make room. They passed by me without making eye contact.

Just as I arrived at the second-floor landing, I was buttonholed by our next-door neighbor, Mrs. Fenner, who was peeking around the edge of her front door.

"Too bad about the game, Zeke. I heard that final play didn't exactly work out the way you wanted it to."

Mrs. Fenner's nosiness often yielded valuable intel, but not at that moment. I speculated as to whether she might be related to Darla Davenport.

A half-dozen ways to answer Mrs. Fenner crossed my mind. I opted for diplomacy. "Mom needs me home for dinner, Mrs. Fenner," I said as I closed the door behind me.

My mother was standing in the kitchen with her back to me. Mom worked as a trauma nurse in the emergency room of Mikan Memorial Hospital. I knew she had just gotten home from work, because she was still in her hospital scrubs. She was on the phone doing plenty of listening, but she wasn't saying much, which was unusual for my mom. Then she said goodbye and hung up.

"Don't bother asking how we did. You're going to be disappointed."

My mom didn't respond.

"Hey, did you see those two marines walking down the stairs? I wonder what that was all about."

No answer.

I set down my gym bag and walked over to the fridge to get a cold drink. When my mom turned around, tears were streaming down her cheeks. Wow, she was taking the loss to Westside a lot harder than I was.

"It's okay, Mom. We'll have another shot at the title in my sophomore season."

My mom gathered herself and brushed away her tears. "That was your father on the phone."

That was weird. My parents had split up six years before, not long after Wade enlisted in the Marine Corps. After Dad moved to Denver, my mom and I rarely spoke to him.

"Those men you saw leaving were from Camp Pendleton. One was a marine captain from Wade's unit, and the other was a chaplain." Mom took a deep breath and rested her hands on my shoulders. I felt her body trembling.

"They drove here to notify us that Wade was killed in action in Afghanistan. Honey, Wade is dead."

That news rattled around in my skull before it sank into the pit of my stomach. It had to be a mistake.

"Wade can't be dead. He's supposed to be coming home at the end of the month."

"I'm so sorry, honey," Mom said. "Your father was telling me how proud he is of Wade for giving his life to his country."

My mom slid down onto the kitchen floor. I sat with her as she wept into a dishtowel until she had no more tears left to give. I was too deeply in shock to do anything more than just wrap my arms around her shoulders and tell her that everything was going to be all right—which clearly it wasn't.

And just like that, a really lousy day turned into the worst day of my life.

5

This Wasn't Happening

A few days later, Mom made the funeral arrangements with the help of a Casualty Assistance Calls Officer from the Marine Corps. I asked her if I could come along, but she said no, she had it covered.

Mothers always seem to know how to handle the difficult stuff, almost like there's some instructional handbook that moms are required to read as part of the whole motherhood deal.

I had never been to a funeral before. There was no way to prepare for my first burial ceremony, no basketball equivalent, no method of reconciling my limitless feeling of loss.

My father drove from Denver to Los Angeles, fifteen straight hours, through the night. It was raining when he arrived at the apartment, in time to pick up my mom and me and take us to the cemetery.

It had been a year since I had seen my dad. He had been a sergeant in the army, a combat veteran of the Iraq War. When he returned home, the doctors said he was suffering from post-traumatic stress disorder. His symptoms included nightmares and flashbacks to the terrible things he had witnessed there.

Dad was dressed in a black suit that was wrinkled and a little too tight on him. He looked tired and obviously hadn't shaved in several days.

No one said a word on the drive to the cemetery. Dad steered the pickup truck into the parking lot at Southland Meadows Memorial Park as a steady downpour pelted the asphalt.

"If it rains on a funeral procession, it means the deceased will go to heaven." It was an ancient superstition that my mother delivered without emotion.

My father threw the truck into park, cut the engine, and stared off into space. The only sound inside the truck cab was rain pinging off the Chevy's pitted hood.

I was dressed in a suit my mom had bought for me a couple of years earlier for a wedding we attended. I had grown four inches since then and was showcasing a lot of sock as I sat on the rear bench seat motionless, sweaty, and lost.

"Maybe we should go inside," I said.

The parking lot was nearly full, and more cars were arriving as my dad circled around to the passenger side, umbrella in hand, to help my mom from the truck. I stood in the rain watching Dad escort Mom to the chapel. After the harsh words they had exchanged during the divorce, I took comfort in seeing them walk together, if only for that fleeting moment.

"Where's the flood?" That was Stretch, weighing in on the distance between my trouser cuffs and the wet pavement below. Stretch was always trying to keep things light. If ever there was a day that needed it, this was the one.

"Knock it off, dude," said Curtis, coming to my defense, just as he had all our lives. Curtis then drove a knuckler deep into the fleshy portion of Stretch's boney upper arm. "That's going to leave a mark, bro."

Flanked by my buddies, I pulled open the double doors leading to the chapel and was stunned to find the mass of humanity inside. There had to be at least two hundred people murmuring and milling around, including about fifty marines in dress blue uniforms.

When I took a step inside, the room fell silent. All eyes were on us. The dank, musty air reeked of decaying wood and burning incense. I wasn't ready for it. Cold beads of sweat assembled on my forehead. I needed to run away. I swallowed hard and turned around to reach for the door handle, but Rebecca's hand intercepted mine.

Tears escaped from her eyes as we walked down the aisle to the front row, where my parents were just sitting down.

"Dad, this is my girlfriend, Rebecca. Rebecca, this is my dad."

My father reached out to shake Rebecca's hand, but she hugged him instead. It was the first time I had seen my dad smile in a very long time.

Rebecca and I sat down alongside my mom. My eyes scanned the surreal scene in front of me. There was an enormous stained-glass window, a half-dozen high-back chairs, and a wooden pulpit.

And a casket draped in the American flag.

With my brother inside.

This wasn't happening. I wasn't ready to let go of Wade. Not yet. Not like this. I felt Rebecca's hand on my arm, and then I heard a voice.

6

Wade Knew the Consequences

"Thank you for being here on this solemn occasion to honor the life of Wade Quentin Archer." It was the marine chaplain I had seen going down the stairs.

I fidgeted in my seat as the chaplain spoke of how Wade was in a better place and now at peace. All I knew was my brother was gone for good and never coming back.

The chaplain concluded his sermon and called upon my brother's commanding officer, a Marine Corps captain, to talk about my brother's military career. As the officer walked to the pulpit, I realized he was the other man I had passed on the stairs on my way up to our apartment. He cleared his throat and surveyed the room.

"Today we mourn the loss but celebrate the achievement of a life cut short but well lived and with purpose," the captain said. "Explosive Ordnance Disposal Technician Wade Archer wanted to be part of something greater than himself, so he stepped forward into danger with tremendous courage and put himself in harm's way for the benefit of others."

I looked over at my parents. My father's eyes were locked onto the marine captain's. Dad's head was rocking gently as if he were trying to commit every word to memory. Mom wore a look of sadness mixed with pride. I could see in her eyes that she seemed to be searching for a way to reconcile the sacrifice Wade had made for his country and his fellow marines.

"Wade knew the consequences of that danger," the captain continued. "He knew that if he fell, the rest of us would carry him forward, forever. Staff Sergeant Wade Archer will always be my brother."

Mine too.

7

I Didn't Know Your Brother Well

In the blink of an eye, the funeral service inside the chapel was over. This is going to sound weird, but I thought I felt Wade's presence in the sanctuary the whole time. It made me wonder whether the fast-break explosion that happened during the basketball game might have been connected to Wade's death.

Mom wept silently into her handkerchief. Dad released a sigh from someplace deep inside.

Rebecca turned toward me and simply squeezed my hand. One of the first things she had ever said to me when we became friends was how much she believed in me. That's what her steady gaze was telling me now. At that moment, I believed I could do anything, even make it through my brother's funeral without being reduced to a blubbering mess.

It got so quiet in the chapel I could hear the sound of bones creaking inside my neck when I tilted my head forward to analyze my socks again. Just when I thought it couldn't get any worse, a man in a sports coat with the cemetery's logo on it adjusted the microphone, sending a blast of feedback screeching through my eardrums.

"At this time, I will announce the names of the casket bearers," Sports Coat Guy said. He pulled a sheet of paper from his inside coat pocket and read the names of six of Wade's Marine Corps buddies. Then the man caught me off guard. "The honorary pallbearers are Ezekiel Archer, Rebecca Tuesday, Curtis Short, Roland Puckett, Brock Decker, and Lawrence Tuckerman."

"Your brother would have wanted your friends to be included," Mom said.

No doubt. Rebecca is my girlfriend. Curtis and Stretch are my best pals. Brock and I had been at each other's throats plenty over the years, but basketball had brought us back together when we enrolled at Jefferson Community College.

Lawrence is a younger kid I befriended at McDerney. He's a math genius who can calculate geographical distances and travel times in his head. He wants to be the mathematics flight specialist on NASA's first-ever manned expedition to Mars. Lawrence also has autism spectrum disorder and almost never speaks, preferring instead to communicate his thoughts with paper and pencil—which can be kind of mystifying and awkward but is sometimes surprisingly helpful. I tried to make eye contact with Lawrence, but he was staring determinedly at his shoes.

They're my crew.

We walked outside as the rain subsided. I watched Wade's marine compatriots guide the casket into a waiting hearse. Then we followed on foot as the black vehicle weaved through the cemetery grounds to Wade's final resting place.

"Sorry for your loss, dweeb."

In case you hadn't already guessed, that was Brock.

"Thanks, man."

"I didn't know your brother well, but I remember him being a way better passer than you—you know, always hitting the open man?"

"Really, Brock?" Rebecca said. "Now is not the time."

Brock was unfazed. "The guy in the cool sports jacket explained to me that an honorary pallbearer receives special recognition but isn't required to do anything," Brock said. "That's a job I'm well suited for."

It was one of those rare moments when cement-head was right about something.

8

I Felt My Shoulders Quake

Seven members of the Marine Corps honor guard standing off in the distance aimed the muzzles of their rifles above Wade's casket, then shattered the graveside silence as they fired a three-volley salute in unison.

My father explained to me that the three-volley salute was a military tradition born out of battlefield ceasefires decades earlier, when combatants would clear fallen soldiers and then fire three volleys to signal that the dead had been properly cared for.

Each volley drove a shockwave through my chest that felt as if it were piercing my heart. I didn't know how much more of this agonizing ceremony I could take. Then another marine raised a brass bugle to his lips. A distorted image of the gray clouds above him was reflecting off the instrument's glossy bell.

My throat tightened as the bugler played a slow and deliberate rendition of "Taps." Everyone in a military uniform saluted the flag covering Wade's casket. Everyone else placed their hands over their hearts.

After the tune ended, two lance corporals from the honor guard lifted the American flag from atop the casket and displayed it to mourners. When they snapped the flag's shiny fabric into folding position, the sharp, unexpected sound gut-punched me.

One of the lance corporals folded the flag end-over-end into a tight triangle before presenting it to the other for inspection. He then handed the flag to the marine captain, who walked over to my mom, knelt down, and presented it.

"On behalf of the President of the United States, the Commandant of the Marine Corps, and a grateful nation, please accept this flag as a symbol of our appreciation for your loved one's service to Country and Corps."

My mother clutched onto the flag with one hand and my dad's arm with the other. Mom seemed too stunned to shed any more tears. I felt my shoulders quake and my vision go blurry. There had not been a sadder moment in my life.

We gathered around the chaplain as he said a prayer before signaling the cemetery laborers to lower Wade's casket into the ground. I joined hands with my mom and dad. We watched as the pine box containing the big brother who had taught me everything in my life descended into the wet earth for eternity.

The casket thumped the bottom of the hole and settled in.

The chaplain picked up a shovel, offered a final prayer, and lobbed a scoop of topsoil into the dank abyss.

When the dirt hit its mark, the hollow thud caused my mom's body to convulse. Dad had witnessed far too many military funerals. He didn't flinch.

It was finally over.

9

I've Done the Math

Curtis and Stretch were the first to offer condolences. Rebecca stood next to me throughout the whole ordeal. Even Brock hung around.

"Your brother's lessons will always guide you. That will never change." That was Coach Kincaid. There was never a shortage of wise words coming from our coach. I was both happy and surprised to see him.

"Sorry I haven't been around the gym since we lost," I said.

"It's only one game, and you've had a ton on your plate," Coach said before checking in with Stretch. "You catch your breath yet?"

"Yeah, after my dad took me out for dinner, I was good as new."

Coach turned to Curtis. "How's that ankle, son?"

"Barely raked over, Coach. I'm totally amped about next season."

"What about you, Zeke?" Coach Kincaid said. "Are you coming back to the team next year?"

The season had ended so abruptly, I hadn't thought about it. Deep down, I knew that Curtis would rather be on dawn patrol at Zuma Beach than playing college basketball. He kept on playing for the sake of our friendship. Stretch was getting a low-cost education as a criminal justice major, so he wasn't going anywhere anytime soon. Brock would probably return next season, if only for the chance to antagonize me.

"I guess so, Coach." That was the best I could come up with.

"If you decide to join us, summer drills start in July. Hope to see you then."

Coach Kincaid opened his umbrella and slogged across the wet turf toward his car, dodging headstones as he waved to a man walking in the opposite direction. That man was Chip Spears. He was headed right for us.

"I'm flying the store's flag at half-staff today in your brother's memory," Chip said.

The store was Chip's Sporting Goods. It wasn't the biggest or best-stocked sporting goods store in town—that distinction belonged to retail juggernaut Global Mega-Sports—but Chip had earned our devotion with his commitment to local youth sports.

Years ago, when Chip learned that my brother had joined the Marine Corps and shipped off to boot camp, he drove to the rec center and dropped off a brand-new basketball, telling me that Wade would make it back to Los Angeles before the guys and I could wear it out. That ball is weathered and frayed and still in the rec center's ball rack.

I guess Chip was right after all.

"What are your plans for the summer?" Chip asked.

There was a lot of interest in my summer plans. "Maybe working out with the team at Jefferson. Why?"

"Business always skyrockets in the summertime," Chip said. "I could use an extra set of skilled hands in the store. Need a job?"

"I guess so—I'll need to check with my mom."

Wow, did that ever sound lame!

"You're eighteen, dweeb." *Oh, great.* Brock had heard me and agreed with my own estimate of my lameness. "Man of the house now. I think you can make that decision for yourself."

Chip shook my hand and told me to think it over.

The rec center director, Vernon Shields, was next to offer words of solace. He had been the basketball coach for the Jackrabbits of Jefferson Community College for twenty-five years before retiring and passing the torch to Coach Kincaid. I figured Mr. Shields had taken over at the rec center to stay close to basketball.

"Your brother was my friend. I don't know what else to say." That was plenty. Mr. Shields was a man of few words. He always made the most of them. "I'm going to need some help around the rec center this summer. Are you gentlemen available? I can't pay you like Chip, but I have it on good authority that there will be other rewards."

"Lunch included?" Stretch said.

"Don't be such a Jake, dude," Curtis said. "Count us in, Mr. Shields. *All* of us."

All of a sudden, I had a busy summer in the works, most of it revolving around the game.

The mourners had begun to disperse when a scruffy kid two or three years younger than me made his way through the crowd.

"Sorry for your loss, butt," the kid said.

"But what?" Brock said in response.

"Butt. Two *t*'s. It's Welsh for *friend*," Rebecca said. "He's being friendly."

The kid spoke with a weird accent, sort of British, but with something in there I couldn't place. Welsh, apparently.

He seemed familiar to me. When I shook his hand, I remembered. He was the kid who drop-kicked a three-pointer the length of the court after I had air-balled the most important shot of my life to date. He was wearing the identical leather boots, loose-fitting trousers gathered at the knee, and bow tie that he had on at the regional championship.

"Say, didn't you—"

Just then, I felt a tap on my shoulder. "Zeke, I'm sorry we have to meet again under these circumstances." It was Chett Biffmann, owner of Biffmann Self-Storage, the place where Wade had stashed his pickup truck when he was deployed.

I turned back. Drop-kick kid was gone.

"Thanks, Mr. Biffmann."

"Call me Chett, young fella," he said with a Southern drawl and a wad of chewing tobacco bobbing behind one fleshy jowl. "Can you stop by Biffmann Self-Storage world headquarters? I've got something I need to give you."

"Thanks, Mr. Biffmann, I'll ride my bike over there in a couple days."

When Chett left, I heard the sound of a commotion coming from around Lawrence and his best friend, Nathan Freeman. The duo had met the previous summer at an internship program at NASA's Jet Propulsion Laboratory in Pasadena. They had become fast friends, though whenever I saw them together, Nathan was angry and, of course, did most of the talking.

Nathan was having a heated, one-sided argument with Lawrence. I went over to break it up.

"What's going on, gentlemen?" I asked.

"I was explaining to Lawrence that the Domenico Lorenzo Ponziani Opening is an inferior chess gambit to the one conceived by Ruy López de Segura," Nathan said as the veins in his neck staged a mutiny above his shirt collar.

What would a military funeral be without tactical chess gibberish? "What's the problem?" I said.

Nathan said Lawrence had handed him note after note with the same words written on them. He showed me one of them:

I've done the math.

"What math?" I said.

"*Exactly my point!*" Nathan screamed.

I wondered whether the funeral had taken too high an emotional toll on Lawrence. "You all right, buddy?" No response. Lawrence rocked from side to side and didn't make eye contact. "Nathan tells me you've been writing some unusual notes. Care to share one with me?"

Lawrence was wearing a pocket protector with seven No. 2 pencils, all freshly sharpened, beveled, and pointing toward the heavens. He removed one, scribbled a note, folded the piece of paper in half, and handed it to me.

I opened it. Lawrence's handwriting was efficient and precise, the letters carefully crafted and tilted to the right. The graphite had smeared in the light rainfall, but the note was legible. I read it silently.

I've done the math.

"What math? What are you talking about?"

Lawrence pulled another piece of paper and repeated the process. I unfolded the note.

Wade's not dead. I've done the math.

I took a long, long pause, looking my friend straight in the eye. "Not funny, Lawrence."

Lawrence wrote me another note.

I'm not joking.

I glared at him. It felt as if the anger raging inside me would turn the rainwater in my hair into steam billowing from the top of my head. I shot a command at Nathan. "Please take him home. Now!"

And that was how my first-ever funeral service ended. I was as confused and distraught as I was before it got under-way. My father took my mom and me back to the apartment before he got on the freeway and drove back to Denver.

10

I Plan to Send You a Sign When I Get There

Mom and I tried hard to get things back to normal. She returned to work at the hospital the next day. I put Lawrence's strange words out of my mind and our friendship on hold as I returned to Jefferson to finish up the spring semester, marking time over the next few weeks until final exams so I could spend the summer at the rec center shooting hoops with Curtis and Stretch to escape my troubles.

I rode my bike home on the last day of the semester and carried it up the apartment stairs.

"I hope you're not going to goof off this summer playing that *basketball* with those hoodlum friends of yours." Mrs. Fenner didn't mince words. She knew exactly how I shouldn't be spending the next three months of my life.

"That's good advice, Mrs. Fenner. I'll give it some thought."

I walked into the apartment to find a note from my mom that said dinner was in the fridge and Chett Biffmann had called asking for me.

Shoot. I had completely forgotten about Chett telling me at Wade's funeral to stop by because he had to give me something. I jammed back down the stairs and rode the five miles to Biffmann Self-Storage "world headquarters." Even though he had only the one location, Chett said he liked to call it that because it sounded impressive. No doubt the storage facility had been important to Wade: he had trusted Chett with his cherished vintage pickup truck.

As I approached the entrance, I noticed a small group of people standing by the side of the building next to some shopping carts filled with junk and covered in plastic.

Those people appeared to be homeless.

I knew from riding my bike around the city and seeing it with my own eyes that Los Angeles had many thousands of homeless citizens living on the streets and in shelters, plus in cars, campers, lean-tos, and in tents under freeway overpasses. It was a full-blown crisis for which our city officials had few answers. It made me realize how fortunate I was to have my own bedroom in my own apartment.

I rode up to the front door and lowered my bike's kickstand. Just then, an old man approached me. He was dressed in tattered clothing and smelled as if he hadn't showered in a long while. I thought he might be with the other people nearby who seemed to be living on the streets.

As I walked toward the door, the man held out a plastic cup and smiled.

"Spare change for some food?"

When I looked into the man's eyes, I began to have one of those *What would Wade do?* kind of moments. For as long as I could remember, my brother was always lending a hand to someone less fortunate. When he coached my park league basketball team, he taught us to always help up a player who fell on the court—no matter which team he played for.

I reached into my pocket and pulled out everything I had in there, which wasn't much, just a few coins. I dropped them in the old man's cup. He smiled as I walked through the front door.

"Where you been, padnah?" Chett Biffmann hawked a wad of brown spittle into a brass spittoon on the floor behind the counter. It made a thumpy splash when it landed. "I hope those people out there weren't bothering you."

It was no bother to me, but I had a feeling Chett Biffmann thought their presence near the entrance to the building was having a negative effect on his business.

"I got a message that you wanted to see me, sir?"

"Tarnation, son! I don't usually see you without that darned basketball in your hands," Chett said, his chin jiggling beneath his gray, tobacco-stained beard.

"Yes, sir."

Chett turned and bent down—revealing about a mile and a half of buttock cleavage that to this day I am unable to unsee—and spun the dial of his floor safe. He lifted the handle, swung the door open, and pulled out an envelope. My name was written across the front.

"Here you go, buddy boy."

"Who's it from?"

"Your brother, the marine. When Wade returned the Chevy after you 'borrowed' it for that confounded road trip to Kansas with that squirrely friend of yours—what's that boy's name? Larry? Anyway, he asked me to give this to you if, well, you know . . ." Chett's voice trailed off.

I stuffed the envelope into my back pocket. "Do you think it'd be okay if I sat in Wade's truck?"

"Space 1046—through that door, hook a right, last row in the back." Chett reached into the safe a second time. "You'll need this." He handed me the key to Wade's padlock.

"Thanks, Mr. Biffmann."

I rode my bike across the storage facility grounds to space 1046, removed the lock, and flung open the roll-up door. The scent of stale gasoline hung in the air as I flipped the light switch. There it was, Wade's prized 1965 Chevrolet Fleetside shortbed pickup truck, hidden beneath a weather-beaten canvas tarp. I pulled it off to reveal the Chevy's gleaming, seafoam-green paint job.

The pickup hadn't always looked that choice. It was a total beater when my dad bought it from an old army buddy. Dad and Wade had restored the truck from the ground up in the carport behind our apartment. I learned to drive it by watching Wade work the three-on-the-tree gearshift whenever he took me to the rec center for hoops practice.

I pulled the chrome door handle, hopped in, and bounced on the soft leather upholstery a couple of times. There was that feeling again. I had sensed it for the first time inside the cemetery chapel and again now, right there in the front seat of the pickup.

Wade's presence.

I slid the envelope out of my back pocket. I had no idea what I would find inside. I tore it open and found a letter from Wade. My skin tingled. I could feel my body temperature rising. .

Dear Zeke,

If you're reading this letter, it means that things didn't go as well as I'd hoped in Afghanistan. I know you're real sad about that.

As understatements go, that was a biggie, I thought.

Maybe it will help if you knew the reasons why I joined the Marine Corps.

I didn't think anything could help me shake the feeling of anguish lodged deep in my bones, no matter what Wade's reasons were for joining.

I wanted to be a part of something bigger, in a place where everyone believed in the importance of walking in the footsteps of our forefathers. I also believed that inno-cent lives must be protected, even if it meant putting myself

*in harm's way to get it done, for the good of the world and
no matter the odds.*

*The corps is all those things, a brotherhood that lasts
forever, that will last long after you read this letter, because
there are no ex-marines.*

*This might seem like a reach to you, but I believe you
have something kind of similar in your life with your
friends. There is an unbreakable bond between you and
Curtis, Stretch, Lawrence, and hell, even that cement-head
Brock Decker. You've always got each other's back, no matter what. The truth is, we're only as strong as the company
we keep.*

It was a stretch for Wade to include Brock in there with
the other guys, but I gave my brother some leeway because he
was talking to me from the hereafter.

*You've got a whole bunch more responsibility on your
shoulders than you did before you got this letter. That
means you'll have to look after Mom and help her move
past the grief. Try to keep an eye on Dad too. I know
that the awful things he saw in Iraq make it nearly impossible for him to be a part of our family for now, but
do your best to stay in touch with him and keep him in
your life.*

*Never forget that the rec center is where you learned the
game of basketball. It's important that you help out Mr.
Shields whenever you can. The kids who go there need your
guidance and support.*

I know I don't need to tell you to keep working on your game. Basketball helped shape the kind of person you are today. The game will continue to serve you as long as you uphold its principles of teamwork and fair play. And remember to always hit the open man.

I wondered for a brief moment whether Brock had secretly put Wade up to writing that part, but I shook off the thought. Impossible.

When I was recovering from my combat injuries last year in Los Angeles, it was real easy to see how much you and Rebecca care for each other. She's a keeper, little brother.

I was crazy about Rebecca but was still trying to figure things out. I had a sense it would take a lifetime—not just for this relationship but for all my relationships.

All of this leads to the main reason why I'm writing this letter to begin with. My most valuable earthly possession is my Chevy pickup. It's yours now. Don't grind the gears, change the oil every 3,000 miles, and don't drive it over 125 mph.

The last part referred to the time when I had driven Wade's truck well in excess of 125 miles per hour to the University of Kansas on a date with destiny. This requires a brief explanation.

Not long after I met Lawrence at McDerney Continuation, he used the ancient Greek geometric technique of neusis construction and seven No. 2 pencils to create a heptagonal device that could intercept communiqués from the Entity, an interdimensional energy being that likes to call itself the 7th Dimension. I realize this must sound odd, but it only gets weirder.

The 7th Dimension had established itself in the intertwined root systems of the world's trees, where it lives today as a singular energy being using the planet's three trillion trees as antennae for its global communications network.

The 7th Dimension brought basketball to the world in 1891 through its secret emissary, the game's inventor, Dr. James Naismith, as a means of fostering peace and brotherhood on Earth.

Basketball succeeded in its intended purpose for well over a century. But over time, violence and greed had taken over the game. The breaking point came when I punched out a ref at the city finals. After that, the 7th Dimension set a firm deadline for taking away basketball for good.

Lawrence caught wind of the decision and learned that the 7th Dimension's headquarters were located in the roots of a grove of trees living adjacent to Allen Fieldhouse, the basketball arena at the University of Kansas. So, we busted Wade's truck out of Biffmann Self-Storage and drove halfway across the country in a race against time to save the game.

Once we arrived, I had to negotiate saving the game with the arena janitor. He later identified himself as the modern-day incarnation of Dr. James Naismith, sent to Earth by the

Entity to handle important basketball affairs, including delivering me the news that the Entity had withdrawn my consideration for a basketball guardianship on its behalf.

Anyway, the truck's speedometer topped out at 125 miles per hour, but I was pretty sure we had the Chevy doing at least 130 as we cut a path across the Great Plains.

Last thing is a heads-up: I plan to send you a sign when I get there, wherever "there" is.

That final paragraph made the hairs on the back of my neck stand at attention.

Semper Fidelis, little brother.
Wade

I yanked on the sun visor, and a set of keys clattered down into my lap.

11

You Need to Get a Job

I picked up my bike and set it into the truck bed. Then I slid the key into the ignition, pushed down on the clutch, and pumped the gas pedal a couple of times—just the way Wade had whenever he took me to basketball practice.

I turned the key.

Silence.

The world was against me. Just when I thought my life couldn't get more complicated, I had inherited an antique truck I couldn't use because I couldn't get it started.

"Pop that hood for me, will ya, son?" It was Chett Biffmann. He had driven up in the Biffmann Self-Storage golf cart, the one with a custom-mounted car battery on the rear bumper. Chett walked over to Wade's truck carrying a set of jumper cables. "I had a feeling this monument to nineteen-sixties automotive technology wouldn't turn over."

I released the hood latch to raise the pickup's metal hood. Chett clamped the cables onto Wade's battery.

"Give her a try."

The engine hacked and wheezed. *Tucka-thuck, tucka-thuck, tucka-thuck, tucka-thuck, tucka-thuck, tucka-thuck, tucka-thuck . . . Vroooooooom!* And roared back to life.

"I think I'm going to take her home, Mr. Biffmann. I appreciate your looking after her when Wade was overseas."

"I'd tell you to change the oil every three thousand miles or so, but I reckon Wade's letter probably covered that. Be safe out there, son."

I eased the truck out of space 1046 and waved goodbye to Chett as I nervously inched across the Biffmann Self-Storage parking lot and headed for my apartment.

It was the first time I had been behind the wheel since I borrowed Curtis's car to take my driving test and get my license shortly after returning home from the trip to Kansas. My mother insisted I get my license because she didn't want a teenage lawbreaker living under her roof. And since Mom didn't have a car and rode the bus to work every day, I never had another chance to hone my driving skills.

The fuel gauge indicated the truck was low on gas. I was flat broke, so I drove straight home and parked it in the carport behind my apartment building.

When I walked into the apartment, Mom was asleep on the couch, courtesy of a double shift at the hospital. She woke up when I pulled open the squeaky refrigerator door.

"Where's your bike?"

"I need to put some oil on that door hinge."

"Not on your life," Mom said. "It's the only way I have left to keep track of what you're up to. Second request: Where's your bike?"

"I left it in the back of Wade's truck."

"I'm going to need more information than that."

I handed Wade's letter to my mom. She put on her glasses and read every word, pausing now and again to gain control over her emotions. When she had finished, she went to the kitchen to make a cup of tea. Mom let the kettle shriek longer than usual before turning off the gas. I wondered if she allowed it to wail like that so she wouldn't have to.

"You know what this means, right?"

"That the water is really hot?" I said, hoping to break the tension and make her smile. It worked.

"Yeah—and the other thing too."

I didn't know what was coming next, but I had a feeling it meant growing up a lot faster than I wanted to. "Does it mean I have to change the oil every three thousand miles?"

"It means you need to get a job. You need to pay for gas, maintenance, and insurance."

I had been afraid that was coming, and it spelled trouble. I doubted there was a local company out there looking for a junior college point guard with a solid mid-range jumper, questionable decision-making skills, and unreliable transportation.

12

Without That Job,
I Was Sunk

I pulled my bike from the rear of the truck and pointed it toward Chip's Sporting Goods. There was no way I could drive Wade's truck there without car insurance and enough gas to make it back home.

It was sweltering outside. I arrived at Chip's in a sweaty heap. Chip was working the cash register, and there were several customers in line, so I wandered over to the basketball section to check out his latest gear. A couple of minutes later, I felt a tap on my shoulder.

"Can I help you, young man?"

For some reason, Chip didn't seem to recognize me. "It's me. At my brother's funeral a couple of months ago, you asked me if I needed a job."

"Did you get that in writing?"

"No, sir." I sensed there might be a lesson buried in there somewhere.

"Did we shake on it?"

Boy, Chip was really putting me through the wringer. "I think so."

"Good. A man's handshake is his word. And his word is his bond. You'll need to schedule an interview."

"Sir?"

"A job interview. You'll need to schedule it."

I wasn't ready for that one. "I've got some time right now, Chip."

Chip sized me up with a keen eye before telling me I was underdressed and too sweaty for an interview. That was true, but I really needed the job, so I went for it. "Could you make an exception?"

Chip raised one of his dark, bushy eyebrows. I couldn't tell if he was annoyed or amused. "I don't give out a lot of exceptions. Are you sure you want to use yours now?"

"Yes, sir."

"Come with me to the office," he said as he tossed the cash register key to an employee stocking the shelves in the chess-and-checkers section. It was Nathan. I didn't know he was working there. Nathan seemed enraged as we walked by.

I followed Chip into his office at the rear of the store. The walls were cluttered with team pictures and wooden plaques commemorating Chip's numerous charitable contributions to local youth sports. He extended his hand to me. "Hello, Chip Spears. Glad to meet you."

That was weird. "Chip, it's me, Zeke," I said as my hand met Chip's.

Chip released his grip and wiped his hand on his Chip's Sporting Goods polo shirt. I was still sweaty all over, including my hands.

"That was like shaking hands with a warm, dead fish. If you're going to make it in the business world, you'll need a better handshake than that."

There was no one around to teach me the finer points of a proper handshake, because my dad had left the family before I was even a teenager, and my big brother had taken off for the Marine Corps shortly after that.

I wiped my hand discreetly on my pant leg, then reached out to Chip a second time. When his hand met mine, I squeezed it so hard, I could hear his knuckles cracking.

"Good lord, Zeke! You're not crushing a can of peaches. Be firm, but not overpowering."

"Yes, sir."

"Let's try that again," Chip said. "Grip my hand, and with friendly sincerity, look me in the eye and smile. Three pumps, three seconds."

After we had cleared that hurdle, Chip handed me a clipboard with an employment application and a pen attached to it. "Fill this out."

Chip shuffled through some papers on his desk while I scanned the application. *I've got this*, I thought. I filled in all of my personal info.

Special Skills? I wrote down ball-handling, free-throw shooting, and running the fast break.

Employment History? That was a cinch. I had never had a job, so I left that section blank.

References? Another easy one. I jotted down Coach Kincaid, Mr. Shields, and Chett Biffmann. They would vouch for me, for sure.

I handed back the clipboard to Chip. He studied my application for what seemed like several weeks, wheezing and groaning louder and louder as he made his way to the bottom of the page.

"You left the Employment History section blank."

"Yes, sir."

"Is there a reason for that?"

Uh-oh, I hadn't seen that one coming. "I've never had a job before."

Chip collapsed back in his chair, pressed his lips together, and exhaled, his stony expression causing butterflies to hurtle against the lining of my stomach. Sweat returned to the palms of my hands.

"How am I supposed to hire you if you don't have any experience?"

Chip's logic was impenetrable. He had me in a hammerlock from which there appeared to be no escape. Without that job, I was sunk. I thought about Wade and how disappointed he would be if I were unable to drive his truck and pay for the gas and maintenance.

Then, in that exact moment, I felt it again—Wade's presence in the room.

"How am I supposed to get any experience if no one will give me a job?" It felt like someone else was saying that, but the words were coming out of my own mouth, stern and direct. Chip seemed stunned by my unexpected flash of reason.

"I hadn't thought of that," he said. "It's an excellent point." Chip rummaged through a desk drawer, pulled out a crisp new Chip's Sporting Goods polo shirt, and tossed it across the desk.

I looked at the tag: my size. Chip had a good eye.

"Congratulations, the job is yours. Come back Monday at 9:00 a.m., and don't be late. Nathan will show you the ropes."

"Thanks, Chip. I won't let you down."

And with that, my first lesson in the art and science of the job interview, complete with professional handshake analysis and tutorial, was in the books.

I waved goodbye to Nathan on my way out the door, but he only scowled at me in return. As I pedaled for home to give my mom the big news, I couldn't help but think that Wade somehow had something to do with it.

13

I Test-Drove My New Handshake

"Honey, wake up! You're going to be late for work." Those were the first words I heard the next morning. I looked at my watch in disbelief—8:30 a.m. My first-ever shift at Chip's Sporting Goods would start at 9:00. With no car insurance and almost no gas in Wade's truck, driving to work wasn't an option.

The bike ride would take a half hour under the best of circumstances. If I didn't get my butt out the door in five minutes, the next voice I heard might be my new boss firing me from a job I hadn't yet started.

I threw on my clothes, dragged a comb across my hair, grabbed my bike, and sprinted for the door.

"What about your breakfast?"

"No time, Mom—can't be late."

I didn't know what would be worse, Chip expressing his disappointment over my tardiness or Nathan getting pissed because he had to wait around for our training session to get underway.

I zipped across town at lightning speed, locked my bike at the rack in front of the store, and flew through the lobby. I was met by Nathan, arms crossed and foot tapping the shiny linoleum floor.

"Time clock. Thataway," Nathan said, his thumb motioning toward Chip's office in the back.

I dashed through the store to a rack of time cards. They were alphabetized, so finding one at the top that said ARCHER on it was a breeze. I stuffed it into the time clock. The machine made a loud *click-thump!* I pulled out the card. My eyes widened as I read the clock-in time. A single bead of sweat trickled south from the top of my head and took refuge in my eyebrow.

"That's right, Zeke, it's nine-oh-five." Chip's frown caused narrow, fleshy wrinkles to align across his substantial forehead. It was not the face of a happy man. "Are you sure you want this job?"

Fair question from the boss. I wasn't sure I actually wanted it, but there was no doubt I needed it if I were ever going to take my girlfriend out on a date in Wade's truck.

"Yes, sir. Sorry. Won't happen again."

"Best not to keep Nathan waiting. He was in a bad mood *before* you walked in late." I found Nathan standing in the exact same spot at the front of the store. He did seem irked.

"Chip said I have to show you how to stock the basketball section," he said. "Let's go."

I already knew where the basketball section was, so I took a couple of steps in that direction when Nathan smacked me on the back of my head. It wasn't a hard smack, just a minor attention-getter.

"What'd you do that for?" I asked.

"You need to show some respect," Nathan said. "I'm supposed to train you, but I've got a lot of my own work to do, so you showing up late is disrespectful. Don't do it again."

Wade used to tell me how important it was to rely on and get along with his fellow marines whenever he was deployed.

"Okay, I get it," I said.

Beyond being Lawrence's best friend, Nathan was captain of the Jefferson Jackrabbits chess team. In a tactical chess game, he was rumored to be able to think as many as twenty-one moves in advance.

Last semester, at the California community college chess championship, which I covered for the school newspaper, Nathan was locked in battle in the middle game when he conceded the title match—even though neither player appeared to my unpracticed eye to own an advantage.

Nathan's decision to resign cost Jefferson its chance at the state title. It was also Nathan's first collegiate tournament loss. When I approached him for a postgame interview, he told me to get lost and stormed away.

Then there was that one super-strange thing about Nathan. It was even weirder than Lawrence having freeze-dried chili mac 'n' beef every day at McDerney because he believed he was in training for a mission to Mars. Nathan carried around in his backpack small pieces of bread baked into the shape of chess pieces. No one knew why. If Lawrence had any insight, he wasn't sharing it.

Nathan showed me how to take inventory of the basketball gear and restock the shelves with backup equipment from the storage room next to Chip's office. I was three hours into my four-hour shift when I heard a pair of boots clomping up behind me.

"Hello, butt." It was the kid with the Welsh accent and crackerjack dropkick who had paid his respects at Wade's funeral. He was wearing the same peculiar clothing. "Can you direct me to the rugby aisle?"

Rugby isn't as popular in Los Angeles as basketball, baseball, football, and soccer, but the store carried a respectable selection of rugby equipment because Chip took pride in meeting the needs of all his customers.

I had learned from a sports history book I checked out of the library a couple of years ago that rugby folklore puts the game's invention in the small town of Rugby in England's Midlands in 1823. As legend had it, one day during a public-school soccer match, a schoolboy named William Webb Ellis picked up the ball and took off running, setting into motion the invention of a whole new game.

The book went on to say that serious rugby historians dismissed the claim as myth because there was no concrete evidence to support it.

"Follow me," I said to the strange kid, who, after that third encounter, was starting to weird me out. When we arrived at the rugby section, I confronted him. "I don't mean to sound rude, but perhaps you can tell me why we keep running into each other."

The kid extended his hand to me, so I test-drove my new handshake—three pumps, three seconds, just as Chip had taught me.

"Ellis, William Webb—at your service."

(14)

Destiny Calls

I tried to respond, but my throat felt as if two hands were squeezing it from the inside. I was on the clock, so I knew I had to pull myself together or risk getting canned on my first day.

If the kid standing in front of me was the ghost of William Webb Ellis, I didn't want to know about it. And if his appearance was the 7th Dimension's handiwork again, I didn't want any part of it.

I tried to change the subject and managed to stammer out the first words that popped into my head. "You looking for a rugby ball?"

"Actually, mate, I'm looking for you."

"Why are you loitering in the rugby section?"

I whirled around. Great, it was Nathan.

"You're supposed to be working over in basketball."

Even though Nathan and I held the same rank of part-time trainee sales clerk, it was already clear that he felt entitled to boss me around, and he seemed to enjoy it too.

"I was helping a customer," I said as I motioned to the kid behind me.

"What customer?"

I whirled around again. The kid was gone. He must have vaporized. That was the only reasonable explanation.

"He was here a second ago." I squeezed my eyes shut and opened them again, hoping for the impossible. No luck. I felt the blood drain from my face. I seemed to be losing my grip on reality.

Nathan channeled his inner Chip Spears: "Quit screwing off, Zeke. Are you sure you want this job?"

"Dunno, bro." It was Curtis, to the rescue. He must have walked in during all the confusion. "But I'm pretty sure he *needs* this job to haul me and my board to Zuma in his brother's jalopy this summer. Gas is expensive, Nate."

"What are you doing here?" I was glad to see my friend.

"Need some traction. I heard Chip carries Huey's Choice board wax. Stuff is epic."

Nathan seemed unhappier than usual as he stormed away. There always seemed to be a cloud hanging over his head. I felt sorry for him.

"Dude's pretty aggro," Curtis said. "Maybe he should take up surfing. Might help him chill."

I decided to test my sanity. "Did you see a kid in funny clothes walking out the front door when you came in?"

"Hard to say, bro. Unless he was wearing an aloha shirt

and board shorts, I wouldn't have noticed him. What time's Chipper springing you?"

"In about half an hour. Why?"

Curtis had a weathered surfboard and a dented 1968 Plymouth Belvedere station wagon with a roof rack and a half-tank of gas. He lacked only a wingman on that sunny afternoon. "Destiny calls. Heavy sets, top-secret spot north of Zuma. Outside break, my man. Huey digs it there."

"Huey? You mean the guy who makes the board wax?"

"Sort of—Huey is the Surf God, the mythical spirit responsible for sending up the gnarly waves."

"Oh, *that* Huey."

"Pick you up at one sharp—and heads up, Becca's comin' with. We'll grab her on the way."

I figured the fresh air would do me some good after my encounter with the phantom from rugby past. I asked Curtis if Stretch would be joining us. Curtis said Stretch was busy helping out his dad with the family painting business. Mr. Puckett was struggling to keep Puckett Painting afloat, so Stretch felt duty-bound to assist. That didn't leave much time for basketball—or anything else.

Nathan rang up Curtis's board wax at the cash register, and Curtis took off. I finished up my work, clocked out, and waved goodbye to Chip.

Nathan caught me by surprise, fist-bumping me as I headed for the door. "Good job, rookie. See you tomorrow." It was a rare moment of congeniality for the chess czar.

When we pulled up in front of Rebecca's house, she was

standing by the curb, all set to go. She greeted us with a wide smile and a basket of sandwiches.

"Shotgun!"

"Nice try, Rebecca," I said, hopping out and opening the door to the back seat with what I hoped was a gallant flourish. "You can't call shotgun when you're the last person to be picked up. It's a rule."

"For a guy making up life every day on the fly, you sure have a lot of rules," she said. "I've never heard that one." She jumped into the front and scooted over to the middle of the bench seat next to Curtis. When I got back in, she took my hand in hers and flashed a big smile. "Isn't that better?"

That was what life was like with my girlfriend.

15

Cartwheeling into the Watery Abyss

We cruised westbound on Interstate 10 and maneuvered through traffic onto the Pacific Coast Highway, heading north. There was a lot of sandwich munching going on, but not much conversation.

Curtis seemed to be entering his mental surfing zone. I had seen the basketball equivalent of it back in high school and during our freshman season at Jefferson, when he would rain three-balls on beleaguered defenders.

Rebecca ate in silence as well. I sensed there was something on her mind, but I let it pass for the moment, knowing she would tell me at some point. Instead, I downed my sandwich, American cheese on egg bread. She knew it was my favorite.

Curtis drove about a mile past Zuma Beach's main parking lot, hung a U-turn, and pulled his station wagon into the only open spot along the highway.

"Righteous parking karma," he said.

When we got out of the car, Curtis climbed into his wetsuit, pulled his surfboard from the roof rack, and threw his backpack over his shoulder. Then we made our way down a foot trail to the shoreline.

Curtis's clandestine stretch of sand was desolate. There were no sunbathers or lifeguard stations, or even any cellphone service, just a couple of surfers up the beach sitting on their boards, floating atop the glassy water.

Rebecca and I set our towels down at a prime viewing spot. I took off my high-tops and felt the hot sand gripping the bottom of my feet and spreading between my toes. There was nothing in front of us but vast, blue-black ocean and boundless sky.

And Curtis, with his sun-bleached, shaggy hair flowing in the warm breeze. He paddled out about a hundred yards, straddled his board, and waited. I knew Curtis would always rather be out surfing than on any basketball court, but sometimes we make sacrifices for our friends. Curtis knew that we relied on him for moral support and his ability to, as Stretch would say, put the biscuit in the basket.

I was sitting hypnotized by the gentle surf when Rebecca brought me back to Earth by kicking sand at me.

"If Chip finds out you got sand on my new polo shirt, he's going to—"

"I'm moving to Kansas," Rebecca said.

My sense of calm dissolved. "You're what?" That didn't make any sense. Why would Rebecca move to Kansas when I lived in Los Angeles?

"There was all that talk about how great the university was after you and Curtis and Stretch got back from the tournament there last year."

The guys and I had won a three-on-three high school basketball tourney in Los Angeles that qualified us to advance to the Western Regionals at the University of Kansas. We lost in the finals there, but we blabbered on and on about the experience for weeks.

It had clearly made an impression on Rebecca. When all of us enrolled at Jefferson Community College, she signed up for courses in the college's Kinesiology Department and started working as a sports medicine trainee for the basketball team.

"I enjoyed the classes at Jefferson so much that I applied to KU's Department of Health, Sport, and Exercise Sciences—and I got in. I'm enrolling there in the fall."

That was a lot of information to process. I tried not to let too much time pass before responding, and all I could muster was, "That's great." It's hard to talk when you've been punched in the stomach.

"Try not to sound too enthusiastic."

Was it that obvious? Just when things were going okay with Rebecca, she tells me she's leaving town. I was tired of losing people—first, my dad moving to Denver, then Wade being killed in action in Afghanistan (although not, according to Lawrence), and now my girlfriend moving 1,600 miles away.

"Don't worry," she said. "We'll stay in touch."

Famous last words.

Rebecca put her hand on my shoulder, but I brushed it off. I hung my head and stared at the sand and surf in front of me, searching for the right thing to say.

Then something caught my eye. The tide receded a lot more than it had earlier.

I looked up at Curtis, who was out far beyond the relative safety of the shallower inshore water. He was on his belly, furiously paddling his board out to the open ocean as a massive wall of water formed in front of him. I couldn't tell if Curtis was trying to catch the rogue wave or get out of its way.

As Curtis reached the base of the rolling beast, he grabbed the nose of his surfboard and pirouetted ninety degrees to face it down. But he seemed to miscalculate his predicament. Curtis's board went vertical. He went over the falls, freefell down the face, and was sent cartwheeling into the watery abyss.

The whitewash consumed him in a thunderous roar.

Rebecca saw it too. She shot up from the sand and screamed: *"Curtis!"*

16

A Paralyzing Jolt Shot Through My Heart

Curtis's surfboard was tombstoning, bobbing up and down, because the leash was either still connected to him or wrapped around an underwater rock. The only visible sign of my best friend was his polyurethane foam grave marker.

Then things went from bad to worse. The surfboard detached from Curtis's ankle. The whitewash carried the board toward the shore and deposited it at our feet. I picked it up and gave it a quick once-over.

The leash was still attached, but the cuff was gone.

So was Curtis.

I glanced at Rebecca, who wore a look of terror on her face as she scanned the ocean's surface for any sign of our friend. I could feel my heart pounding against my chest. I started to hyperventilate and felt suddenly lightheaded.

SMACK!

Rebecca had slapped me across the face. It hurt more than when Lawrence did the same thing twice the year before on our road trip to Kansas in Wade's truck.

"Get ahold of yourself!" she screamed. "We need to do something!"

It was unclear what Rebecca wanted us to do, but it seemed like it wouldn't matter after I saw a dorsal fin darting straight to the spot where Curtis had gone under. The menacing creature circled one time and plunged below the surface, its tail fin spraying seawater in all directions as it submerged.

Tears were streaming down Rebecca's cheeks. "It's a shark!" she screamed.

Call it heroism or call it utter stupidity. I tore off my polo shirt, flipped my wallet and cell phone onto the towel, and hauled butt for the water. The frigid Pacific stung my bare skin when I barreled in. I drove my arms and flailed my legs, propelling my body against the strong current in a race against time to save my friend.

The sport of basketball has a term for what I was attempting to do: a full-court buzzer-beater.

Blindfolded.

As I approached the area where Curtis had disappeared, I recalled the terror I had felt the first time I watched *Jaws* on late-night television, when frolicking children playing in the shallow waters of Amity Beach sent a signal to the movie's sea monster about the presence of its next meal.

I felt my lips quivering, thanks to the effects of the icy water on my skin. A shooting pain cut across the lower part of my body. It wasn't a shark bite. It was my leg muscles cramping. I dipped below the surface to look for any sign of Curtis or the shark, but the saltwater stung my eyes, and I could see nothing. I floated back up.

It had already been at least a couple of minutes. Curtis was gone, and so was the shark. A paralyzing jolt shot through my heart as feelings of fear and hopelessness engulfed me.

Curtis was dead.

And I was a sitting duck.

17

Dispatch the Rescue Squad!

My mind flashed to all the times Curtis had bailed out our basketball team by nailing a rainbow jumper from distance when we needed it most. Or the lunch periods in the McDerney cafeteria when he had stepped between Brock and me to keep us from clobbering each other. It was time to return the favor, and there was nothing I could do.

Rebecca stood at the water's edge, waving her arms frantically and screaming something I couldn't make out. I cupped my hand to my ear in an attempt to amplify the sound.

"Behind you!" she yelled.

I looked over my shoulder in time to see a gigantic wave coming right at me. I ducked under the water, hoping it would pass overhead, but I got caught up in what Curtis had once referred to as the "washing machine," when a surfer gets rolled around underwater by a breaking wave. The force of the wave shoved a gulp of seawater down my throat, causing me to exhale the remaining air from my lungs.

I fought the swirling current with every ounce of strength I had. I drove my body to the surface and gasped for precious oxygen. Then, in what Stretch would have referred to as "calling the walrus," I tossed up my sandwich.

I dog-paddled to stay afloat, with no game plan beyond clinging to life. I felt a gnawing emptiness in my gut.

There was no hope. Out of sheer desperation, I closed my eyes, and in the dark shadows of my mind, I prayed for help from anybody or anything that might be listening.

It must have worked.

Curtis's body shot straight up out of the water. He landed face first, motionless. I swam toward him as fast as I could. Another wave hit me, but I fought it off and flipped Curtis over. He was in one piece and his wetsuit was intact, but his skin had turned dark blue. It didn't look like he was breathing.

"Hold on, buddy. Nobody drowns on my watch," I said as I hooked my elbow under his chin and made a beeline for the shore. Just then, something else came shooting out of the water. It was the sea creature. It breached and glided across the surface of the ocean right in front of us.

It wasn't a shark.

It was a dolphin.

The dolphin lobtailed, lifting its flukes out of the water and smacking them down onto the surface with a loud slap. It clacked and grunted as it swam back out to sea.

With the help of the surging current, I got Curtis to shore. Rebecca took over and pulled him onto the sand. His body was cold and lifeless. The cuff was still wrapped around his ankle.

Rebecca placed her ear next to Curtis's mouth and nose to see if he was breathing. She looked up at me and shook her head. Then she checked his pulse. Still nothing.

"Call nine-one-one!"

I picked up my cell phone and focused my burning eyes on the screen.

"No bars. I'm going to have to make a run for it."

I laced up my high-tops with shaking hands as Rebecca performed CPR on Curtis. I had learned about CPR in health class at McDerney. Rebecca's knowledge, however, was far more advanced. She applied repeated compressions to Curtis's chest in an attempt to restore his circulation and breathing. After a short while, she pressed her lips against Curtis's to force air into his lungs.

I looked to the south in the direction of the public beach. It was inaccessible because of the jutting cliffs and boulders piled high along the shoreline. The only way to summon help was to go straight up to Pacific Coast Highway.

I sprinted for the road and tried to flag down one of the passing cars, but no one was stopping. I took off running for the public entrance to the beach, a mile away. A sharp spasm under the lower edge of my ribcage staggered me, but I fought off the pain and kept going. I flew across the parking lot straight for the lifeguard station.

"It's my friend! We pulled him from the water, but he's not breathing!"

"Where is he?"

I was too winded to speak, so I pointed to the north.

The lifeguard keyed the microphone on his handheld walkie-talkie and radioed for help. "Los Angeles County Fire, we've got a surfer down. Lifeguard needs assistance. Dispatch the rescue squad! Zuma Sector B!"

The lifeguard plucked a set of keys from a hook on the railing. We tore across the sand to a nearby Jeep, jumped in, and retraced the path back to Curtis's secret surfing spot.

My ears picked up the sound of a wailing siren. By the time we had made it to where Curtis's station wagon was parked, a Los Angeles County Fire Department ambulance was waiting for us, lights flashing. Two emergency medical technicians pulled a stretcher from the rear of the ambulance and followed us to the beach.

When we got there, Rebecca was still applying compressions to Curtis's chest.

"We'll take it from here, miss," said one of the paramedics.

Rebecca must not have heard him, because she didn't stop. "C'mon, Curtis. Breathe, dammit!"

"Young lady!"

Just as she pulled her hands from Curtis's chest, his body convulsed, and he coughed up murky seawater.

He was alive!

The EMTs gently pulled Rebecca off Curtis, placed an oxygen mask over his nose and mouth, and checked his heart rate with a stethoscope. Then they did something I knew would make him unhappy, at least if he lived through the ordeal: they took a pair of trauma shears from a medical bag and cut away his prized wetsuit.

Ouch, that's going to leave a mark, Lawrence would have written in a note had he been there.

I hugged Rebecca while the paramedics covered Curtis with a blanket and strapped him onto the stretcher for the trip to a hospital. Rebecca was drenched in perspiration and could barely stand.

"You did great," I said. "You saved him."

The paramedics and lifeguard whisked the stretcher up the hill. We gathered our belongings and followed close behind. The EMTs pushed the stretcher into the ambulance and radioed ahead: "Mikan Memorial, this is LA County Fire triple seven. We're coming in hot from Zuma Sector B. Drowning victim. Do you copy?"

Mikan Memorial? That's where my mom worked as a trauma nurse in the emergency room.

The hospital dispatcher crackled a response: "Copy that, triple seven. Standing by."

"I want to ride with Curtis," Rebecca said to me.

The lifeguard overheard her and had a brief conversation with the paramedics. The crew helped Rebecca into the back of the ambulance, flipped on the siren, and floored it.

I fished the car keys out of Curtis's backpack and wondered what the future would hold for my best friend after spending . . . how long? It must have been more than two minutes of his life, without oxygen, submerged under the surface of the ocean.

18

There's No Easy Way
to Say This

Curtis's station wagon was easier to handle than Wade's truck because it had an automatic transmission instead of the pickup's clunky, three-on-the-tree gear-shifter. Since I didn't have car insurance, my plan was simple—sit on the gas pedal and try not to hit anything or anyone on my way to the hospital.

My mom had worked at Mikan Memorial for as long as I could remember, so I knew my way there like the back of my hand. I screeched into the hospital parking lot, grabbed Curtis's backpack, and raced through the emergency department's double doors. The waiting room was jam-packed.

"I need to see my friend!" I blurted out to a woman shuffling papers at the information desk.

"That depends." The woman kept shuffling and didn't look up.

"On what?"

"On what your friend's name is." Good point. I was so frazzled, I hadn't mentioned it.

"Curtis Short. There was an accident at—"

"Clandestine beach just north of Zuma. Yes, I heard. You must be Ezekiel. I'll phone your mother."

The woman picked up the receiver while I surveyed the waiting room. There were little kids coughing and grownups wrapped in bloody bandages, but no sign of the oxygen-deprived waterman with the lethal jumper.

The door to the trauma area swiveled open. Out walked Rebecca. I could see she was really upset—her hands were shaking, and her eyes were red.

"Is he okay?" I asked.

"He was unconscious when we arrived. The doctors hooked him up to a bunch of machines."

I once saw Curtis put on a shooting clinic in a postseason game while playing on two sprained ankles. He poured in thirty from downtown without breaking a sweat that night. I was certain this near-drowning thing was no match for him.

"Did you call Curtis's sister?"

Rebecca nodded.

"What did the doctors say?"

"They asked me how long he was underwater."

"What'd you tell them?"

"I told them I didn't know," she said. "I lost track of time."

So had I. I figured Curtis was submerged for a couple of minutes, maybe longer. But he was in outstanding physical condition, and Rebecca had been able to get him breathing again, so I thought chances were he would be all right.

"Just before Curtis slipped back into unconsciousness on the ride here, he whispered something to me. The siren was blaring, so I could barely make out what he was saying. I think he was hallucinating from lack of oxygen."

"What did he say?"

Just as Rebecca started to answer, I caught a glimpse of Stretch walking toward us across the emergency room. Best friends were getting to be in short supply, so his presence was welcome.

"Curtis said he thought I had surpassed Brock Decker as the guy on the team with the choicest haircut. Is there a stat for that?"

"How did you know to come here?" I asked.

"I picked it up on my trusty police scanner," Stretch said. "'Drowning victim, top-secret surfer's beach north of Zuma.' Curtis told me he'd be there, so I put my superior detective skills to work."

Stretch's law enforcement credentials were thin. They consisted of his ambition to work as a private eye and his status as a freshman criminal justice major at Jefferson. It was news to me that he had a police scanner.

"What do we know?" Stretch said.

"Not much. I'm hoping my mom comes out soon, so we can find out what's going on."

Stretch was wearing a painter's cap and stained coveralls that were several inches short of their intended southerly destination, so I figured he had been on the job with his dad when the news came over the scanner.

"Don't worry about Curtis. I owe him some money, so I know for a fact he'll pull through." Stretch, as usual, was trying to lighten the mood.

Stretch reached down with his boney index finger and motioned to an unoccupied corner of the waiting room. "Got a second?" he said. The grin on his long face faded to a grave expression, which was unusual for a guy who found the silver lining in everything. I sensed it might be bad news. I followed him into the corner.

He hesitated, as if he were weighing his words. "I hijacked the Puckett Painting van to get here. It won't be long before my dad notices it's missing, so I've got to make this quick."

"Please, no more bad news today," I said. "I can't handle it."

"Sorry about that," Stretch said. "There's no easy way to say this. I've got to quit the team and drop out of Jefferson. I already told Curtis this morning."

Stretch said his dad told him that business had been lousy for several months. If he didn't come to work for the company full time, Puckett Painting would go bankrupt, and the family would lose everything.

I took a step backward to weigh the gravity of Stretch's words and sat down. I didn't know how I would find a replacement seven-foot-two best friend who told bad jokes and knew how to run the pick and roll. I slumped back in my chair and felt a lump forming in my throat.

I had started the day by almost losing my job. I was already minus a father and down a brother. Curtis was hanging ten on death's doorstep. Stretch was swapping a basketball for a paint roller. My girlfriend was leaving town to attend the same Midwestern university that had rescinded my basketball scholarship.

What else could go wrong?

I looked up and saw my mom walking out of the trauma room. She was headed right for me, and I knew that look.

19

All Roads Lead to Lawrence

"Honey, are you all right?" Mom forced a smile, but her eyes gave her away. They always did.

"I'm okay. How's Curtis? Is he going to make it?"

"How long was he underwater?"

A lot of medical professionals were asking that question, so I knew it must be important.

"Dunno. Couple of minutes, maybe. Why?"

My mom wiped the perspiration from her forehead with the palm of her hand. Deep down, I always knew that her job included delivering bad news to the family and friends of unlucky people lying on hospital beds on the other side of that door. But I had never witnessed it in person—until that moment. Mom spoke with a kind of cold compassion I had never seen in her before.

"Curtis is suffering from brain hypoxia. That's when the brain is cut off from oxygen long enough for the body's major systems to begin to shut down." I felt Rebecca's grip tighten on my arm. "That's why the doctors are trying to figure out how long he was underwater. It'll tell them what to expect."

Mom explained that brain hypoxia was really serious. Curtis's brain cells needed an uninterrupted flow of oxygen to function properly. She said the shortlist of complications ran from pneumonia to brain damage to a permanent vegetative state.

"There are a couple of important factors for the doctors to consider—Curtis's overall health and the level of oxygen in his blood when he went under."

A little bit of sunlight was peeking through the dark clouds. Curtis was a stud. *He's got this*, I thought.

"We're going to hang out here until Curtis wakes up," I said.

"No, honey. The doctors won't know anything for twenty-four hours. You kids go home and get some rest. I'm going to work a double shift, so I won't be back to the apartment for a while. I'll call you if anything changes."

I gave Curtis's backpack to my mom. She hugged us goodbye and went back through the trauma room door.

When we got to the station wagon, there was a parking ticket pinned to the windshield. In my mad dash to the hospital, I had parked Curtis's surfmobile in a handicapped zone.

"You should ask Chip to make out your first paycheck to the City of Los Angeles Department of Transportation," Rebecca said. "It'll save you a trip to the bank."

I laughed with relief. Rebecca's joke was the first sign that the shock of Curtis's near-death experience was starting to wear off. We were buckling our seatbelts when we saw Curtis's sister whiz past us in her car. She parked near the emergency entrance and sprinted inside. I was glad my friend would have family in his corner. I started the station wagon.

"I need to tell you what Curtis said to me on the way here."

I cut the engine. "What did he say?"

"I was so freaked out by it that I asked the EMT for something to write with. I didn't think I could rely on my memory, so I wrote it down word for word."

Rebecca handed me a folded-up scrap of paper. It reminded me of how Lawrence would relay urgent 7th Dimension intel the previous year when we were saving the game of basketball from extinction. I read the note silently.

The dolphin, like, communicated with me. Freakiest thing ever. Said to tell Zeke that all roads lead to Lawrence. Then it totally saved my life, dude.

20

There's a Problem with Lawrence

It was the second time in as many hours that Rebecca had given me too much information to process. Rebecca moving to Kansas was straightforward bad news. Her note relaying Curtis's ambulance message was a puzzle. Rather than a mystery solved, it was more like a mystery deepened.

The lack of oxygen to Curtis's brain had no doubt played tricks on him. And I still had no idea how he had launched himself high into the air while he was seconds away from certain death.

Curtis had mentioned months earlier that he felt a strange kinship with dolphins after so many encounters with them while riding the waves. He said he could have sworn there were times when a dolphin would lead him to the sweet spot where a wave was about to form. Dolphins love to surf, he said. He had seen them do it lots of times. Curtis said it was the reason why he had changed his major at Jefferson from philosophy to oceanography after our freshman year.

Lawrence had been my point man on the trip to Kansas, doing double duty as math wizard and geography genius. Without him, no way could I have rescued basketball. So, it seemed plausible that all roads still led to my astronaut-in-training autistic friend.

"What do you think it means?" Rebecca said.

I didn't answer. I was still trying to figure out myself how a dolphin could know that Lawrence had bailed me out before it passed along that information to Curtis telepathically. Nothing was making sense.

"Are you *listening* to me, Ezekiel?"

Uh-oh. Whenever Rebecca called me by my entire first name, I knew it was time to pay attention.

"I am listening. I'm thinking it's probably some kind of surfer's code. I think it's best we ask Curtis if . . . I mean, *when* he recovers."

Rebecca didn't respond. She didn't have to. Our friend was up against the wall, and we had more questions than answers. I started Curtis's station wagon again and drove in rush-hour traffic to Rebecca's house. Not another word passed between us until we arrived at her house, and I eased the car to the curb.

"I don't want to be alone right now," she said.

I wasn't expecting that. "I guess I can hang out here with you for a while."

"My moron stepbrother's probably lounging around, watching cartoons with Jed. It's their favorite summertime activity. I don't think I can deal with it right now."

That seemed reasonable. Brock had a knack for showing up where he was least wanted. And our two forwards often traveled together—on and off the court. "I guess we can go to my house."

"Okay."

A few minutes later, I pulled into the carport next to Wade's pickup, and Rebecca and I walked up the stairs. I was hoping to avoid an encounter with Mrs. Fenner, but nothing was working in my favor that day.

"Where are you two going?"

"My apartment, Mrs. Fenner."

"Does your mother know you're bringing a girl in there?"

"She's not a girl, Mrs. Fenner. She's my girlfriend. We really have to go now." I shut the door behind us a little harder than usual.

Rebecca seemed amused. "She's only trying to protect you."

That was a point of view I hadn't considered. I figured Mrs. Fenner was just being aggressively nosy, as usual, as the apartment building's self-appointed busybody-in-chief. Maybe my mom had secretly put her on retainer to keep an eye on me.

"I see you're strong in American cheese," Rebecca said as she peered into the refrigerator.

Like father, like son. American cheese was my dad's favorite snack, so naturally, it became mine too. Stretch once noted that if Mrs. Fenner ever sentenced me to house arrest, I would have enough American cheese in the fridge to survive until my parole hearing.

Rebecca made sandwiches, I poured soft drinks, and we shared dinner on the sofa. When we finished, I tried to pick up our conversation on the beach where we had left off before we almost lost Curtis.

"University of Kansas, huh? Cool place to learn and play basketball and stuff. I almost made it there once. If there's anything I can—"

Rebecca covered my mouth with her hand. She brought her index finger to her lips with the other hand.

"*Shh.*"

When she removed her hand, she kissed me, so I had a feeling she wanted me to stop talking. Then she pulled a blanket over us. We hung out together on the sofa and didn't talk for the longest time—and in those moments, I had never felt so close to another human being in my life.

Bam! Bam! Bam!

The sound of pounding on the front door jarred us awake. Wow, Mrs. Fenner was taking her role seriously, I thought. Rebecca wrapped herself in the blanket and tiptoed to the bathroom.

BAM! BAM! BAM!

There was more pounding, this time harder and more deliberate. I squinted through the peephole. Even though it was dark outside, I could see that it wasn't Mrs. Fenner, which was a relief. But the person standing outside looked angrier than Mrs. Fenner ever did.

It was Nathan.

"Open the door, rookie!"

I thought I saw steam coming off the top of Nathan's head as he bounded through the doorway.

"Was I supposed to turn in my polo shirt at the end of my shift?"

"Have you got a girl in here?"

I thought Nathan was only allowed to boss me around when we were on the clock. Showing up at my apartment unannounced to investigate my personal life had to be some sort of Chip's Sporting Goods code violation.

"Why didn't you use the doorbell?"

"Because I'm in a bad mood."

Nathan explained that when he took the bus to Lawrence's house for their weekly chess match, Mr. Tuckerman said Lawrence hadn't come out of his room since Nathan's last visit. "Lawrence just kept asking his dad to shove more paper under the door."

"Why?"

"I guess he's writing a lot." That wasn't much of an answer from Nathan, but then again, it wasn't much of a question. "Mr. T said you're the only person he'll listen to. I don't know what makes you so special, so I rode the bus here to find out."

There seemed to be no end to Nathan hassling me. I told him to wait outside while I used the bathroom.

Except for the quality time I had just spent on the sofa with my girlfriend—and which Nathan had so rudely interrupted—I wondered how much weirder and crummier the day was going to get.

"Nathan says there's a problem with Lawrence," I whispered to Rebecca. "I've got to go." Rebecca gave me a hug and told me she would lock up and get a ride home from Brock.

I grabbed the keys and my jacket and took off down the stairs with Nathan.

"You *sure* you ain't got a girl in there?"

I was sure of just one thing—my road at that moment was leading straight to Lawrence.

21

I Need You to Write
This Down

I parked the station wagon in front of the Tuckerman residence.

"I think I'll wait in the car," Nathan said. "I don't want to be there when you pry open that bedroom door after it has been sealed shut for seven days."

"Suit yourself."

I hurried up the walkway and rang the doorbell. Even though there was no answer right away, I elected not to pummel the door with my fist the way Nathan had at my apartment. Best to focus on the desired outcome.

Lawrence's father eventually answered. He looked gaunt and haggard, as if he hadn't slept or eaten in a long time.

"Hello, Mr. Tuckerman. Nathan mentioned that Lawrence has been holed up in his bedroom for a little while. I thought I'd stop by to see if there was anything I could do."

A look of relief washed over Mr. Tuckerman's face. He pressed the palm of one hand to his heart and offered the other one to me. I saw it as an opportunity to practice my new handshake. I looked Lawrence's dad in the eye and smiled—three pumps, three seconds.

"Lawrence respects you," Mr. Tuckerman said, "especially after you trusted him enough to take him on that road trip to Kansas."

The trusting part had been a process. Lawrence had snuck into the back of Wade's pickup moments before I hit the highway. I didn't notice he was back there until I hit top speed on Interstate 15 outside of Barstow. At the time, I was on a strict deadline to reverse the 7th Dimension's decision to take away the game, so there was no turning back.

"Down the hall, to the left."

Lawrence was an only child. The hallway walls served as a timeline of family photos, beginning with toddler Lawrence and his parents visiting libraries, planetariums, and space museums. Lawrence's mother was in most of the pictures, up until the moment when she had killed herself in the family kitchen a couple of years earlier, so the last few had only Lawrence and his dad in them. I was reminded that, beyond his autism and wayward genius, Lawrence had had a lot to deal with in his short life.

I tried the doorknob. It was locked. "Hey, Lawrence, it's me, Zeke. How's it going in there?"

I heard some rummaging around inside. I looked down and saw a folded-up piece of paper at the base of the door. I picked it up and read it.

Hey, Zeke. It's me, Lawrence. How's it going out there?

Good grief. "Lawrence, I'm here to help you. If this is how we're going to figure this thing out, it'll take us a long time." I was already losing my patience. If Nathan were standing there with me, he would've blown a fuse by then. Another note soon followed.

What's the password?

"We don't have time for this!"
I heard Lawrence scribbling again. He pushed yet another note under the door.

Bingo! You got it on the first try.

I heard Lawrence flip the lock. He whipped open the door, muttered, "All roads lead to Lawrence," and slapped me hard across the face—in the exact same spot where Rebecca had slapped me hours earlier. Then he slammed the door and locked it again.

My face stung as if someone had whacked it with a hot skillet.
"Why'd you do that?"

Another note. I wondered how much longer it would go on before Nathan lost his patience and drove Curtis's station wagon through the Tuckerman front door.

If more people greeted their friends this way, there would be fewer friendships. The ones that survived would be stronger.

It was unique logic from the pencil maven, who seemed to be speaking from experience. I wasn't aware of any other friends Lawrence had except for Nathan, who would've thrown a haymaker at Lawrence in response to being slapped. But I was still standing there, so maybe Lawrence was onto something.

He unlatched the lock. When he swung the door open, all five of my senses were engulfed by a week's worth of Lawrence Tuckerman brainpower unleashed in a small room with the windows closed. I was grateful there was an adjacent bathroom, or it would have been a lot worse.

I stood in the dimly lit hallway blinking my watery eyes. I was not prepared for what I saw. Every square inch of Lawrence's bedroom—floor to ceiling—was covered with white sheets of paper connected together by masking tape.

Lawrence had written what appeared to be a massive mathematical equation on all of that paper. It was a sea of digits and math symbols that circumnavigated the room in an endless flow of unharnessed intellect.

It started on the top of his wooden desk. Once that was covered, the paper chain made a move for the floor and over to the base of the wall. It circled the bedroom from baseboard to ceiling, then went round and round up there like a vellum tornado until the ceiling was completely covered. Next, it darted down from one corner of the room to the carpeting, where it spiraled around like fallen dominoes until there was no open space anywhere. Even Lawrence's bed was covered.

"You're just in time." Lawrence actually said those words out loud instead of writing them down. We were making progress.

I took two steps inside the room. The paper floor tiles crunched beneath my feet.

"Watch out!" Lawrence pointed to what must have been the final link in the mystery chain resting in the center of the floor. "That's my conclusion!"

I shot Lawrence a quivery smile. It seemed as though my brainiac friend had finally gone over the cliff. I felt it was best to play along so I wouldn't agitate him any further. "What conclusion would that be?"

"Get a pencil," Lawrence said with a faint glimmer of a micro-smile, since every pencil in the room, all seven, resided in his pocket protector. "I need you to write this down." He handed me a pencil and what was likely the last unused piece of paper for a city block.

"What is all this?" I said.

"Advanced biomathematics."

"What's that?"

"The use of mathematical models to help understand phenomena in biology."

"Oh." I had learned to give Lawrence ample legroom whenever he was springing an advanced theory on me. "Why

don't you give me a little more information? I'd like to understand it better." Meaning, I'd like to understand it better than
I did, which was not at all.

"Start writing. I'm pretty sure I've proved that human consciousness is not tethered to the human brain."

Those words rolled off Lawrence's tongue as if he were
ordering a burger at a fast-food drive-thru window—no emotion, just clarity. It made the hairs on the back of my neck
wiggle.

"*Pretty* sure?"

"Yeah. Pretty sure."

22

I Felt My Skin Get Clammy

I followed Lawrence's instructions and began writing down his words. Human consciousness? Check. Not tethered to human brain? Check.

Lawrence mumbled more and more sci-fi gibberish using complicated, multisyllable words I had never heard before. I wrote it all down until I ran out of space on my allotted sheet of paper, front and back. I was so caught up in capturing the words that I hadn't thought about their significance.

I set down my pencil. "What does it mean?"

"It means I've done the math. Wade's not dead."

"I know. You told me that at his funeral." Lawrence was talking in circles. I was worried he might go down a rabbit hole he could never escape from. I tried to change the subject. "Why'd you ask me to write everything down?"

"No reason."

"*No reason?*"

"Yeah. No reason. I wanted to give you something to do, so you could feel like you were accomplishing something. I learned it in special needs school. The teachers would ask me to write everything down. They did it to keep me busy."

"Did it work?"

"Yeah, for a while, until they ran out of paper."

That put us back at square one. I had no idea where our conversation was going. I felt certain Nathan must be ready to pop a blood vessel in his neck by then. But there was a silver lining: I had managed to get the air circulating in Lawrence's bedroom again, and I was able to verify he was not in imminent danger, despite his precarious mental state.

"When you told me that all roads led to Lawrence, you were right, buddy, because here I am," I said. "I have to go before Nathan marches in here and puts me in a headlock."

I held out my hand for a parting fist bump, but Lawrence only stared at it. I took one last look at the towering paper sculpture and wondered whether Lawrence had any idea how far from the real world he appeared to have drifted. The resulting sadness left a heavy feeling in my chest.

I was walking down the hallway when I heard Lawrence deliver his parting shot.

"I'm looking for patterns where there aren't any," he said. No doubt.

I said goodbye to Mr. Tuckerman and made my way to the station wagon. When I got in, Nathan glared at me.

"Any luck?"

"Tough to say. He had a lot on his mind," I said, trying to downplay the severity of Lawrence's departure from reality.

"Did he say anything about playing chess again?"

"Not exactly, but I have a feeling he'll be ready for you the next time you set up the board."

I drove Nathan home and went back to my apartment. I plopped down on the couch, exhausted from what felt like the world's longest day—work, beach, Curtis in the ICU, Rebecca's warmth, Nathan's anger, Lawrence's meltdown. I was grateful I didn't have to work the next day, because it would give me a chance to rest and visit Curtis in the hospital.

I closed my eyes. The next thing I knew, there was a blanket covering me and the sun was peeking through the curtains. It was morning. I saw a note from my mom on the kitchen table.

> Good morning, honey. You were sleeping so soundly, I didn't have the heart to wake you. There's oatmeal on the stove. I'm going in to work early so I can help monitor Curtis's vital signs. I'll call you if anything changes.
> Love,
> Mom

I was reaching for the phone to check in with Rebecca when I noticed the answering machine's red light flashing. I pushed the play button. The automated voice said the message had been received at eight o'clock the previous night. I must have slept through it.

"*This message is for Ezekiel Archer. Zeke, Coach Kincaid here. Jefferson's athletics department just notified me that they're going to paint the inside of the gym much sooner than originally planned. That means I've got to move up team try-outs to tomorrow morning at nine a.m. Sorry about the short notice. See you then, and don't be late.*"

Was Coach testing me?

I looked up at the clock. My eyes must have been bulging out of their sockets. I felt my skin get clammy.

It was 8:45 a.m.

23

Run It Again!

I threw on my gym clothes, grabbed the keys, and zoomed out the door. If Mrs. Fenner had been loitering in the hallway, I would have applied a flying body press before she could get any words out.

A few months earlier, I would have pedaled my bike at top speed all the way to Jefferson. But there were new options available. When I got downstairs, those options were parked side by side in the carport.

On one hand, Wade's pickup truck was nearly out of gas and unlikely to start because of its unreliable battery. On the other hand, Curtis's Plymouth wagon had plenty of gas in the tank, but it didn't belong to me. And since I had no car insurance, I wasn't legally allowed to drive either one.

I chose the wagon. It offered the best chance to get to the gym on time, and I could imagine Curtis's faint voice in the back of my head saying, *"No problem, bro—say hi to Coach K for me, and gas her up when you're done."*

I hit bumper-to-bumper traffic, a ritual of commuting during rush hour in Los Angeles. Chamberlain Drive, the main route to the college, was a parking lot. It made me sad to see homeless people living in tents all along the route.

I finally made it to Jefferson's main gate at the corner of West Way and Baylor Boulevard. I parked the car and jammed across campus for the gym. As I approached the entrance, the sight of a gawky mass of spindly limbs stopped me in my tracks.

It was Stretch. He had on the same paint-stained coveralls he had been wearing at the hospital the night before. He was hoisting a long ladder onto the roof of the Puckett Painting van. Stretch's dad was behind the wheel.

"I thought you quit the team."

"You're late for tryouts, Mr. All-Conference."

"What time is it?"

Stretch looked at his watch. "It's nine-oh-five. I heard that Coach called tryouts for nine a.m. sharp. I wonder how many laps that'll cost you guys. Brock's not going to be happy."

"What are you doing here?"

"I came by to tell Coach Kincaid I was dropping out of college. After that, my dad and I took measurements and prepped the gym walls. Puckett Painting got the job."

"Wow, that's great." I said the words, but my heart wasn't in it. Stretch asked for an update on Curtis. I had no news to pass along.

I said goodbye and pulled open the gym's double doors. It

was the first time I had ever tried out for a basketball team without Curtis and Stretch. I felt alone even though a couple dozen guys were running layup drills.

When I stepped onto the court, everyone froze.

"The easiest part of making this team is walking through that door on time," Coach Kincaid said, his voice bouncing off the arena walls.

I heard Brock Decker and Jed Swagerty snickering. Beads of sweat formed on my forehead. I didn't want to use what had happened to Curtis as an excuse. I also didn't want to complain about Coach's last-minute notification of the scheduling change. So I decided to get out in front and take my medicine.

"How many laps, Coach?"

"Fifty." A collective groan rolled across the hardwood. "That's ten laps for every minute you were late."

I set down my backpack and took a couple of deep stretches. "Ready."

"I think you misunderstood me, Zeke. That's fifty laps around the gym for *your teammates*. You're going to stand here and help me count."

That groan turned into a group whine as the players circled the gym in one continuous line of resentment. On the seventh lap, Brock bumped into me on purpose as he jogged by. "Thanks a lot, dweeb."

We spent the next two hours running basic shooting, passing, and dribbling drills. Coach Kincaid wrote notes on his clipboard and made sure we stayed hydrated. Toward the end of tryouts, Coach gathered everyone together at center court.

"Nice job so far, fellas. We're going to work on the fast break and then call it a day."

Coach Kincaid's philosophy of basketball success went beyond the standard belief that games were won or lost at the free-throw line. He felt that a well-executed fast break was the best path to victory because it allowed for the potential to wear out an opponent. He said it also provided opportunities for easy buckets and sped up the overall tempo of the game, which favored the Jackrabbits' style of play.

"But the real reason we're going to rely on the fast break this season is because it's fun to run," he said.

That was comforting news, because fun would otherwise be in short supply without Curtis and Stretch filling the lanes as I drove the ball down court.

Coach Kincaid split everyone into two groups and selected five players from each to take the floor. I was thankful that Brock and Jed were on the other squad.

Coach instructed the players on offense to run a set play. When someone missed a shot, it would trigger the fast break. "Rebounder, get the ball to the point guard. Two guys fill the lanes, one trails as a safety valve, one hangs back on defense. For this to work, the point guard has to make a good decision. Let's run it, gentlemen."

We gathered at one end of the court, with my team on defense. Jed set up on offense at the point, but when Coach Kincaid wasn't looking, Brock pushed his friend out of the way.

"I'm going to enjoy this," Brock mumbled to me under his breath.

Coach tossed the ball to Brock, who took a one-bounce dribble and buried a twenty-footer before I had time to get set on defense.

"Get a hand up, Zeke," Coach said.

Brock called for the ball back and nailed the exact same shot, that time right in my face. I was surrounded by teammates, but it felt like I was in solitary confinement. I missed my friends. I felt my ribs squeezing me. I was lost.

"Been awhile since I torched you like this," Brock said. "Forgot how good it felt."

Brock set up the offense again. He passed the ball to Jed on the wing. Jed threw up a jumper that bounced off the lip of the rim. One of my guys got the rebound and hit me with a sharp outlet pass. I maneuvered across half court. Brock was hounding my every move. When I pulled up at the free-throw line, I bounced the ball off my foot and out of bounds.

Coach Kincaid blew his whistle. "Run it again!"

I was tired, hungry, and demoralized.

"Nice hands, dweeb," Brock said.

I had been the Jackrabbits' starting point guard the previous season, but now I wasn't sure I would even make the team.

Brock set up the offense again and snapped a chest pass to Jed. Jed passed the ball to their center, who clanked a hook shot, setting another fast break into motion. I worked the basketball up court, with Brock in my jersey. When I arrived at the stripe, Brock swatted at the ball, missed, and cracked me across the jaw with his elbow on the backswing.

I was seeing stars. When my head cleared, Brock was grinning at me.

"Looks like your face got in the way of my elbow," he said. "That's going to leave a mark."

Without thinking, I shoved Brock. I couldn't believe I had just done that. What was happening to me?

Coach Kincaid wasted no time separating us. "Seems like we just went through this with you two," he said. "How about you channel some of that energy into running this play to the best of your ability."

Coach Kincaid retrieved the ball and bounced it to Brock. Then Coach pulled me aside. "How's the jaw, son? Want me to sub you out?"

"I'm fine, Coach. Let's play."

Coach took off his cap and ran his hand through his thinning gray hair. He seemed frustrated.

"You're dribbling the ball at Brock like you're planning to ask him if you can borrow some money," Coach said. "Get your head in the game, Zeke. This team is relying on you."

Coach's warning got through to me. Curtis and Stretch were not going to miraculously walk through those double doors, and Brock would never let up in a million years. I needed to put my head down and make that play happen the way Coach had drawn it up.

"Run it again!"

Coach bounced the ball to Brock, who yo-yoed the dribble as he backed me into a screen at the high post. I fought through the pick and squared up in front of him. When Brock took the shot, I leaped into the air and swatted it, went horizontal for the loose ball, and sprinted down court.

Out of my peripheral vision, I saw two teammates filling the lanes on either side of me. The trailer was moving into position behind me just inside the three-point line. The play was developing with the kind of rhythm and flow I had felt only one time before.

I was running the fast break—*the play*—*perfectly*.

Then, when I pulled up at the free-throw line, it happened.

Again.

24

My Body Was Wracked with Fear

The Jefferson gymnasium went black. My leg muscles tightened. A ripple of fear circled my spine before lodging itself deeply inside my gut.

Not this again, I thought. I hadn't yet figured out what had happened that first time.

I blinked. The light filtered back in. I looked down and noticed that the glossy hardwood had transformed into a gravelly carpet of dirt and sand. My skin broiled beneath the blazing sun.

I was back in the same dusty hole as before, huddled on the floor of the pit, with the basketball still in my hands. The heavy drone of truck engines rattled the dirt walls surrounding me. The acrid smell of diesel exhaust carved its way into my sinus cavities. None of it was making sense.

I lifted my body off the ground to take a look around. Canvas sandbags were stacked in a rectangular formation, reinforcing earthen berms around the opening of what I recognized from watching war movies to be a foxhole. Wade had once said the marines called it a "fighting hole."

I peeked over the barrier. The fighting hole was positioned on top of a hill. I saw five military vehicles on patrol down below. They were Mine Resistant Ambush Protected All-Terrain Vehicles—I knew because Wade used to tell me about them in his letters home. Wade called the military vehicle an MRAP for short.

He said the Marine Corps had selected the Cougar version of the MRAP for use by explosive ordnance disposal companies in Afghanistan because it had the best survivability record of all the combat vehicle choices.

The MRAPs down below were painted desert tan to provide camouflage in the dusty landscape. They had massive guns mounted on them and were moving in formation about a hundred feet away.

Someone shouted a muffled command. Then the center vehicle bucked and blew up right in front of me. The flash from the blast blinded me for a split second. My jaw ached from the pressure wave. People were screaming.

I was in a war zone in the middle of a scorching desert.

When the dust and debris cleared, I could see the MRAP resting on its side. Thick black smoke was pouring from the engine compartment. Two of the MRAP's infantrymen—possibly the gunner and the driver—were sprawled on the ground nearby, their battle fatigues soaked in blood. Neither was moving. The vehicle's third marine was lying on the road unable to run for cover because of what appeared to be a shrapnel wound to his left leg.

"Sweep to me! Sweep to my vehicle!" the wounded marine yelled to his men. A horrific feeling came over me—it sounded like Wade's voice. The remaining four vehicles dispersed and then returned in a serpentine formation toward the fallen marine.

"Leg injury, bring a stretcher!"

As the MRAPs drew closer to the downed marine, the unseen enemy behind me peppered the area with heavy small-arms fire, the sound of bullets zinging past my ears. The marines returned fire, and a fierce gun battle was instantly underway. The wounded marine could only cover his head with his hands, curl into a ball, and wait it out.

A round of gunfire tattooed the ground in a straight line heading right for the fallen marine. The bullets ripped open his chest.

"I'm hit!"

Three marines with a stretcher darted toward the wounded man, but before they could get there, a follow-up volley of bullets seemed to finish the job. His body was lying on the desert sand in a bloody, motionless heap. I took a closer look at his uniform. It had a Marine Corps staff sergeant insignia on the sleeve.

Just like Wade's.

"*No-o-o-o-o-o-o!*" I screamed as I slid back down into the fighting hole. I banged my fist against the dirt wall over and over. Someone was going home from that desolate hell on Earth in a body bag, and there wasn't a damn thing anyone could do about it.

My body was wracked with fear. I needed to get out of there and go somewhere safe, like maybe a basketball court.

Then I felt a tap on the shoulder. I almost jumped out of my skin when I turned around. It was Wade. He was still alive, but blood was spurting across the fighting hole through a bullet wound in his chest.

"All roads . . ." His voice gurgled and trailed off. He coughed up a grisly mix of blood and saliva and spit it on the ground. I pressed my palm against Wade's chest in an attempt to stanch the bleeding.

"What about them, Wade? What about the roads?"

Wade gasped for air. His body shuddered as the life force drained from it. "All roads . . . lead to Lawrence." Then he collapsed onto the ground and died, my big brother, right there in front of me.

After that, everything went black again.

When I regained my senses, I was standing at the free-throw line at the friction point of the fast break. No time had elapsed, and I needed to decide what to do with the ball. I sensed there were teammates filling the lanes around me, but I couldn't make them out, so I rose up and took a jump shot.

The ball slammed off the glass backboard and went straight down through the orange metal hoop.

"No fair, Coach!" Brock shouted in mock protest. "He didn't call bank."

Coach Kincaid whistled tryouts to a close and waved everyone to center court. I stood there in shock.

"Good work, Zeke," Coach said. "I hope you fellas were paying attention. That's the way we want to run the break this season. See you tomorrow for the second round of tryouts."

25

I Felt My Heart Hammering Against My Ribcage

I slid into Curtis's station wagon and drove home. On the way, I tried to process all I had experienced during the surreal moments in Lawrence's bedroom and on that nerve-rattling fast break.

Lawrence had used a mile-long math formula to determine that Wade wasn't dead. After that, Wade had died, right before my eyes, in a freakish desert battle. Then the unthinkable happened: I shot an uncontested straightaway jumper from the free-throw line—and banked it home.

There could only be one explanation: I was losing my grip on reality.

"All roads lead to Lawrence."

Those five words were haunting me. First Curtis says a dolphin communicated this message to him telepathically at the instant he was about to drown. Then my nerd-genius friend Lawrence speaks these exact words in a rare third-person self-proclamation during our bizarre exchange in his oxygen-deprived math cave.

Then comes the capper: I discover in some kind of on-court dream state that those were also Wade's last words before he died on the desert battlefield. Or had I been standing in the fighting hole with the *ghost* of Wade? Or was the 7th Dimension delivering a message I could not comprehend?

"Shouldn't you be at work right now, young man?"

"It's my day off, Mrs. Fenner." Mrs. Fenner was so up in my business, I was halfway tempted to ask her if *she* knew where all roads led.

I was starving and made a beeline for the fridge. On my way there, the answering machine's flashing red light caught my eye. It would either be good news or bad—there no longer seemed to be anything happening in-between.

I pressed play and heard my mom's voice: *"Hi, honey. Great news! Curtis regained consciousness. The doctors are running tests and watching him very carefully because he's still in intensive care. I'm working a double today, so I'll keep an eye on him and call you later with an update. Curtis has been asking for you, but I told him only immediate family members are allowed in the ICU. I love you, son."*

I scrambled out the front door as swiftly as I had walked in. I don't know whether Mrs. Fenner said anything to me as

I plunged down the stairway, because I was traveling faster than the speed of sound and must have outrun her jabbering.

I had no idea what kind of shape Curtis would be in or why he wanted to see me. Since I was barred from the ICU, I probably couldn't find out anyway. It was just as well. I didn't think I could handle any more tragedy.

I parked the wagon and walked to the hospital's main entrance. There was a security guard at the information desk in the lobby.

"What can I do for you, young man?" the guard said. It was the second time someone had young-manned me within a matter of minutes.

"I'm here to visit Curtis Short. I understand he's in the intensive care unit." I thought that saying the full name of the hospital ward would make me sound more official.

I watched as the security guard tapped some numbers and letters into a keyboard, hit the Enter key, and stiffened. "What is your relationship to the patient?"

I moved my nonshooting hand behind my back and crossed my fingers, hoping it would minimize the impact of the lie I was about to tell the guard. "I'm Ezekiel Short. Curtis Short is, um, my brother."

The guard sized me up with a keen eye. No doubt he had dealt with plenty of desperate and deceitful fake family members in his hospital law-enforcement career. He jotted something down and reached for what I thought might be his badge and handcuffs. I was sunk.

"Here, clip this visitor's badge to your basketball jersey, Mr. Short. ICU is on the third floor. Elevator is thataway."

My knees buckled in relief as I entered the elevator and punched the 3 on the control panel. When the door opened, the antiseptic smell brought back emotional memories of the time my mom had taken me to the emergency room when I busted my ankle in park league basketball. I had been frightened by all the bright lights, shiny medical equipment, and doctors and nurses running around everywhere. I had felt like I was letting down my team because I was going to be out of competition for several weeks.

A sign directed me to intensive care. I waved at a woman wearing scrubs at a nurse's station before pulling open the ICU's entrance door and walking in. I felt my heart hammering against my ribcage as I wandered around the ICU ward in search of my friend.

I walked past about a dozen critical patients before I saw him, lying pale as a ghost in a hospital bed. Above and behind him, pinned to a bulletin board, there was a paper sign with the typewritten words SHORT, CURTIS—IMMEDIATE FAMILY ONLY on it.

Curtis's eyes were closed, an oxygen mask strapped across his nose and mouth. Machines were beeping and buzzing everywhere. I walked up beside him. Curtis must have sensed my presence. He blinked and opened his eyes.

I tried to speak, but my throat tightened, and the words wouldn't come out. I felt warm tears gliding down my cheeks.

Curtis said something, but his words were muffled beyond recognition by his oxygen mask. I moved closer, leaned forward, and listened intently.

"Dude."

26

Too Many Questions and Not Enough Answers

I was never so happy to hear the voice of another human being in my life. Curtis looked weak and frail. His face was scraped up, and his shaggy hair was matted together in clumps. His eyes seemed weary. He had an IV line hooked up to his nonshooting arm.

"You okay?"

Curtis nodded and motioned with his finger for me to move closer.

"Does this oxygen mask make me look fat?" His voice sounded muffled, as if he were talking into a canvas bag filled with gym towels.

I chuckled and rolled my eyes to the heavens.

I remembered what my mom had said about brain hy-poxia and how it could possibly lead to brain damage, or worse. I decided to test my friend's mental condition.

"Do you remember anything?"

Curtis pulled down the oxygen mask below his chin and cleared his throat. He took in a couple of deep breaths, as if trying to acclimate his body to the air in his hospital room.

"Dunno, bro. Head's pretty fuzzy right now," he said, "but I do remember that your girl was wearing candy-apple lip balm."

"That's not exactly what I was talking about." It was clear that oxygen deprivation was no match for my friend's ability to recall critical details.

"I felt terrified by the weight of the ocean forcing me down. I was gulping seawater, and I could feel it going way down into my lungs." Curtis paused to catch his breath. "I had no control over what was happening beneath that wall of water." He paused again. "I thought my time was up. I thought I couldn't fight anymore. I remember thinking, I hope surf's up in heaven."

Curtis was struggling to take in air after this revelation, so I pulled his oxygen mask back over his face. Just then, I heard footsteps coming up behind me. It was my mom. She frowned and shook her head.

"You must be Ezekiel Short, Curtis Short's long-lost brother from another mother."

The security guard must've ratted me out for sure. "Sorry, Mom."

My mother took Curtis's temperature, pulse, and blood pressure. She wrote his results onto a clipboard on the wall, adjusted the IV drip, and asked Curtis if he needed anything.

"Nah, I'm good, Mrs. A," he said, forcing his words through the mask.

Mom gave me *the look* and pulled me aside. "Five more minutes, Zeke, that's it," she whispered. "He is *not* out of the woods yet. Curtis needs to rest."

After my mom left, Curtis pulled down his mask again and continued with his tale. He said he was about to black out from lack of oxygen when something smooth and rubbery nudged his face. He told me he opened his eyes and was beak to beak with a dolphin. Curtis said the dolphin spoke to him, but its lips never moved.

"Its lips?"

"Dolphins have two dorsal bursa/phonic lip complexes. It's how they produce sounds." That explanation made it clear he had taken good notes in his Introduction to Oceanography course at Jefferson the previous semester.

Curtis told me the dolphin used its snout to pry him off the ocean floor and maneuver him onto its back in front of the dorsal fin. Then the dolphin shot up to the surface and flipped him out of the water with its flukes.

"Your girlfriend said I belly-flopped and came to rest on top of the water facedown, probably not what the dolphin had in mind. Glad you were there to flip me over and pull me out."

I didn't think Curtis was in any kind of condition to hear about the supernatural experience I had that morning running the fast break, or even that Lawrence had twice expressed to me a message identical to the one that the dolphin had communicated to Curtis. There were too many questions and not enough answers.

Even so, I couldn't help myself. "Rebecca told me what you said about the dolphin while she was riding with you in the ambulance. What do you think it means?"

Curtis didn't answer right away. He motioned for his cup of water and took a long sip from the straw.

"Dunno, bro. I think you'd better ask Lawrence. Only thing it means to me is my guardian angel has two flippers and a tail fin."

27

I'm Not Leaving Till You Open This Door

I slid Curtis's oxygen mask gently back into place and said goodbye.

"Wait," he said as he drew in several deep breaths of the life-giving gas.

"My mom said you need to rest. I should—"

Curtis pulled down his mask again. "That dolphin . . . man, I don't know what to make of that. But you and Rebecca—you saved my life. I owe you guys everything, brah."

Friendship, I had learned from Wade, was a commitment made by two people to look after each other's well-being. I knew in my heart that Curtis would have done the same thing for me. Heck, even Stretch would have, although he would have complained a lot and reminded me about it at regular intervals in the decades ahead.

"How about you get well soon and come back to the team. Coach Kincaid's riding me hard. Without you and Stretch, it's no fun."

"People move on, bro." I hoped Curtis was referring to Stretch quitting the team to help save the family business. No such luck. "You know how I'm always telling you I love basketball as much as I love surfing? Gotta confess it's not true. The ocean is my calling. I only shoot hoops to hang with you dudes."

That news was a knee to the nuts. Deep down, I had known it all along.

Curtis was lucky, and not just because we had saved him from drowning. He had a calling. Surfing wasn't a hobby, or a job, or a career, or even a diversion from his daily life's obligations. He knew exactly why he was on Earth. He was there to surf, to learn and grow from whatever happened while gliding across the surface of the water, and to enrich the lives of those around him with the experience.

I had no idea what my calling would be.

"Better get outta here before your mom comes back. I don't think I could handle the carnage in my delicate condition."

The security guard gave me the steely eye when I handed him my visitor's badge on the way out. I knew the time had come to confront Lawrence about all the weird things that were happening. If all roads truly led to him—and by that point, I had no reason to doubt it—I needed answers, and I wouldn't leave his room until he coughed them up.

I drove Curtis's station wagon to Lawrence's house and knocked on the door. Mr. Tuckerman looked even more unkempt and exhausted than before. Lawrence seemed to have that effect on people.

Lawrence's dad sensed the urgency of my visit, so we dispensed with the formality of a handshake, and I went straight to the last door on the left and banged my knuckles against it. There was the predictable no answer, so I knocked harder.

"Lawrence, it's me, Zeke. We need to talk."

"Go away. I'm busy."

"I'm not leaving till you open this door."

I heard the lock unlatch. Lawrence pulled open the door, screamed, "All roads lead to Lawrence!" and swung at me again with his open palm. I grabbed his wrist in midflight, his hand just inches from the spot where he had landed a blow the day before.

"Our friendship has stood the test of time," I said. "I think it's safe to say you don't need to do that anymore."

When I released Lawrence's arm, he turned around but left the door ajar. I walked inside and closed it behind me. The first thing I noticed was that the smell didn't curl my nose hairs as much as it had one day earlier. The second thing was he had taken down the hundreds of white sheets of paper and stacked them on his desk a foot high.

Then I saw it—again.

The only other time was a year earlier, when Lawrence and I drove to 7th Dimension headquarters near Allen Fieldhouse to save basketball from the scrap heap.

It was Lawrence's heptagonal antenna made from seven interconnected, sharpened, and beveled No. 2 pencils. The homemade device was resting next to the paper stack on his desk.

"Enough people are telling me all roads lead to you, so here I am. I need to know what the hell's going on."

28

Looking for Patterns Where There Aren't Any

Lawrence sat down on the chair of his bedroom science laboratory and hovered over the pencils, eyes closed, head tilted at a forty-five-degree angle.

"What's going on?"

Lawrence raised his hand to silence me but didn't break his concentration. He swiveled his head on its axis as if he were trying to tune his body to a radio frequency.

"You're blocking the signal," Lawrence said. I moved to the other side of the room to give him more space to operate. "I'm getting a lot of static, but I think I can make out what they're saying."

"They?"

"The 7th Dimension."

I was on the doorstep of Lawrence's world. From past experience, I knew it would be bizarre and unpredictable. I would try to keep an open mind, but I sensed it would be more difficult the deeper we plunged.

"See this?" Lawrence pointed to the mountain of paper. "I figured it out. Wade's not dead. I've done the math."

I knew Lawrence's heart was in the right place, but there was only so much I could take. I felt sorry for my friend, for the burden he carried as he explored questions for which there were no rational answers. I felt I had to put a stop to it for my own sanity, but I didn't have the right words, so I decided to just leave. Before I could reach for the doorknob, Lawrence's words froze me in my tracks.

"Seven days without shooting hoops makes one *weak*."

I felt my heart rate accelerate and my palms get sweaty. "What did you say?"

"I didn't say it. Wade did."

Wade used to tease me with that saying whenever I got lazy and skipped basketball at the rec center for a couple of days. It was our own private goofy joke. No one else knew about it. *No one.*

"Tell me where you heard that!" I demanded.

Lawrence opened his eyes and leveled his head. "The 7th Dimension."

"You need to do better than that." I took a seat on the edge of the bed. "Start talking, friend."

The tone of my voice must have made Lawrence uneasy. He picked up a sheet of paper from the stack, turned it over to the blank side, and scribbled something. Then he folded the paper in half and handed it to me. I read it silently.

*The 7th Dimension altered its spectral broad-
cast subcarrier again. So annoying. I recalculated
the coordinates and tapped into the Entity's
revised non-neutral linear half-frequency.*

More gibberish.

Lawrence's mind had sunk a hook into something I couldn't comprehend. I knew he wouldn't let it go. I had learned to trust the pencil sultan, so I was determined to stay there until I got all the answers, no matter how strange they might be. Lawrence wrote me another note.

Advanced biomathematics.

"Yeah, you mentioned that yesterday. What about it?"

Lawrence seemed to calm down. He put his pencil back into his pocket protector. "I was pretty sure I proved human consciousness isn't tethered to the brain. I decided to test my theory using the 7th Dimension's communications network. I took a shot."

Lawrence flashed a faint smile after throwing down what was for him a rare basketball reference.

"Human consciousness?" I said. I was hanging onto our conversation by my fingernails.

"It's a lack of awareness of what you're not aware of."

I tried to break down those words, but it only made my head hurt. Lawrence rocked from side to side in his chair. I could tell he knew I had no clue about the meaning of what he had just said.

"It's your sense of identity in the world, your ability to perceive and experience the sensations around you," he said.

I checked out of our conversation for a fleeting moment to reflect on Lawrence's definition of human consciousness, but he brought me back to the conversation by cracking me across the face! There was a split-second delay before the pain engulfed me. I tried to speak, but he cut me off.

"Your perception of being slapped—the pain, the hot glow on your skin, the indignity—that's human consciousness. Understand?"

Sort of, but the part about it being unshackled from the brain did not compute. It is common knowledge that we perceive the world around us via the brain, and that organ is anchored to the body inside the skull. Period. End of conversation. What Lawrence was saying about human consciousness being untethered wasn't making sense.

I stiffened my posture and threw my hands up in the air. "I don't get it."

"When Wade died, I saw how it affected you. Thought I could fix it. You know, as a friend."

Lawrence explained that when he learned Wade had been killed in action, he barricaded himself in his room and read his biomathematics textbook over and over in search of clues. He said he wanted to find a way to reunite me with my brother so it wouldn't hurt anymore.

"I was looking for patterns where there aren't any. After a while, I figured it out. Maybe."

"Maybe?"

"Yeah. Maybe."

29

I Took a Mental Step Backward to Regroup

My head was swimming—a routine occurrence in Lawrence's presence. Ever since we had met at McDerney Continuation a year earlier, his life seemed to consist of equal parts supernatural gift and near-insurmountable challenge. I had no idea where all that talk of human consciousness was coming from or where it would lead. But if history could serve as an indicator, I was in for a rough ride.

"Physics summer camp," he blurted out.

I recalled that Lawrence had a quantum mechanics internship at Caltech the previous summer, when most kids I knew were doing layup drills in basketball camp.

"That's where it started," he said.

"Uh-huh." Made sense. It had to start somewhere.

"It's complicated."

No doubt that would turn out to be an understatement. Lawrence explained in terms I was barely able to understand that he believed human consciousness was a form of energy that existed as a fundamental element of the universe and outside the constraints of time and space. What's more, he said the scientists at Caltech had taught him that energy could neither be created nor destroyed—it could only change form.

"Wade's brain was like the AM radio in his antique truck," Lawrence said. "It picked up signals and processed them. Similar to how a radio sends processed signals to a speaker, Wade's brain routed signals to his consciousness. When Wade's Earth suit died in that gun battle in Afghanistan, his consciousness changed form. It's a universal law. I was using advanced biomathematics and quantum mechanics to try and figure out what it changed into."

I took it on faith that Lawrence believed what he was saying, but I was secretly asking myself whether he had gone off the deep end again.

"Any luck with that?"

Lawrence confessed that for all the biomath and physics he had immersed himself in after Wade died, he was unable to unlock the mystery of what had happened to Wade's consciousness.

Until the breakthrough.

Lawrence said he was daydreaming when a thought popped into his head. "I had a hunch that the 7th Dimension might hold the answer, so I devised a way to tap back into the Entity's communications system."

The speed of Lawrence's rocking increased. He seemed to grow more and more nervous. He snatched a sheet of paper from the stack and wrote me a note.

Turns out the 7th Dimension's role on Earth is way bigger than basketball.

"What's that supposed to mean?"

Lawrence hovered over the heptagonal device again while I wondered where it was all going to take us. There was more scribbling and hovering. Then he folded the piece of paper in half and pushed his chair away from the desk with his feet.

"I don't know if you want to read that."

"Why not?"

"I don't know if you're ready for it."

That was an ominous warning coming from Lawrence, whose fearlessness up to that point was well documented.

I had taken a leap of faith with him before when we drove Wade's pickup to 7th Dimension headquarters at the University of Kansas to confront the Entity about its decision to take away basketball. I couldn't imagine that anything on that sheet of paper could possibly be as crazy as what we had experienced on that journey.

I stared at that innocent note as if I had found an unopened box of donuts in my gym locker after practice. I knew it might not be good for me, but I couldn't resist the temptation.

Lawrence rocked and fidgeted. His eyes darted around the room but did not meet mine. He was leaving the decision up to me, and it was an easy one, because there was nothing left to lose. I picked up the note and read it in the privacy of my own head.

Dr. Naismith built into the game of basketball a top-secret portal into the 7th Dimension's inner sanctum. It's possible to solve the mystery of the transformation of Wade's consciousness by venturing through that portal, but Dr. Naismith is the only one who can show you the way.

Well, that only made sense if Lawrence had written it while standing on the surface of Mars eating a freeze-dried meal.

I felt clammy and lightheaded. My breathing got shallow. I was drowning in a sea of Lawrence Tuckerman gibberish.

I took a mental step backward to regroup. Lawrence's transcription of the 7th Dimension's communiqué might well have explained what I had experienced while running the fast break at the regional title game at Jefferson and again during Coach Kincaid's tryouts. And if Lawrence's nonsensical words were true, maybe all I had to do to truly understand Wade's ultimate destiny was to run another fast break *to perfection*. No big deal.

"The Entity doesn't like it when I intercept their communiqués. If you tell anyone, I'm sunk," Lawrence said. "The music is not inside the radio."

That did it. I was on sensory overload.

Lawrence's channeling of 7th Dimension transmissions must have syphoned all the oxygen from the room. I needed to get out of there, fast. "Sorry, gotta go."

I took off down the hallway, but Lawrence's words stopped me before I could round the corner.

"Wait, there's more," he said. "All roads lead to Lawrence."

"Yeah, you made that really clear already. And I came to see you." Curtis telling me a dolphin had communicated those words to him was weird enough. But Lawrence referring to himself in the third person was a troubling new development in our friendship.

"Kansas, you idiot. Lawrence, *Kansas* . . . as in the University of Kansas . . . KU, Jayhawk Town."

"Why didn't you tell me that before?" I practically shouted.

"You didn't ask."

30

The Signs Were Everywhere

"I've got to go sort all this out. I'm leaving now," I said.

"Where are you going?"

There would be only one place to go after receiving intel from my friend that pushed the boundaries of reason.

"Lawrence."

"What?"

"No. I need to go to *Lawrence, Kansas,* to look for answers, just as soon as I can clear out some time to travel."

Lawrence's eyes darted all around the hallway but refused to meet mine. "Wait here," he said as he speed-walked back to his bedroom. I heard the shuffling of paper. When he re-emerged, he handed me a folded-up note. I opened it.

Shotgun!

"I don't think so, buddy. I don't even know when I'm going, but I've got to go it alone this time."

Lawrence must have anticipated my rejection of his wingman request. He pulled a note from the back pocket of his jeans.

I could do the mathematical calculations on our way there.

I wasn't so sure I needed that. I had found Dr. Naismith on my own the year before when I gained access to the basketball court at Allen Fieldhouse. Dr. Naismith was disguised as the janitor, but I eventually figured that out.

I tried to let Lawrence down easy. "I don't think your dad has ever forgiven me for the last time we drove to Kansas without his permission."

Lawrence wasn't letting it go. He pulled out another note from his shirt pocket, which was, unusually, empty of pencils.

Who's going to communicate with the 7th Dimension when you get there? You need me.

Nothing Lawrence could have written on those notes would have changed my mind. I valued our friendship too much to put him in any more danger.

"I'll need you to stay here and monitor activities from the command post."

I didn't wait for Lawrence's response. I turned and walked out the front door.

But reality set in when I got back to Curtis's station wagon. Even if I could make the time to travel to Kansas, I had no means of getting there. I doubted that Wade's antique truck could handle another road trip like that, even if I drove it at legal and reasonable speeds. Curtis's Plymouth wagon was roadworthy, but it didn't belong to me. And even if Curtis gave me permission to borrow it, I had no money for car insurance. My mom would ground me till the end of the century.

Even if I found enough loose change under the sofa cushions at the apartment to afford a bus ticket, I had to be at work the next morning. Chip was counting on me, so I couldn't let him down by bailing at the last minute. And there was no telling how worked up Nathan would be when he found out he had to cover for me.

I also had basketball tryouts to worry about. After my shift at the store, I needed to hustle over to Jefferson for day two. I had to make that team, or else. If I were a no-show, there was no way Coach Kincaid would make an exception. He would cut me for sure.

It felt like I was standing at the crossroads again. Technically, since I was behind the wheel of Curtis's station wagon at the time, I was sitting at the crossroads.

For added impact, that stressful moment coincided with what seemed to be a total eclipse of the sun, because the giant yellow ball of glowing gases in the sky was obscured by a colossal egg-shaped object.

It was Stretch's head, covered by his trademark white painter's cap. The rest of him was decked out in coveralls.

He was banging on the window with his paint-encrusted knuckles. The Puckett Painting van was parked across the street.

"Roll it down, Zeke."

I hand-cranked the window earthward. "What are you doing here?"

"I don't have a lot of time. If my dad notices the van's missing, I'll be dead man painting."

Stretch told me he had snuck off during his lunch break to visit Curtis at the hospital.

"How'd you get past the guard?"

"Private investigators are always thinking on their feet. I told him I was Curtis's older brother, Stretch Short, and I was there to slap a fresh coat of paint on the ICU. I could tell he didn't believe me, but he seemed so amused that he handed me a visitor's badge and pointed toward the elevator."

Stretch said that when he asked Curtis if I had been by there to visit, Curtis started talking nonsense, saying something about talking dolphins and how all roads led to you-know-who—or, as I now knew, you-know-*where*.

"It's weird how Lawrence's name has been coming up a lot lately," I said.

"After that, all the machines went haywire and a bunch of nurses rushed in. I think Curtis might have slipped back into a coma."

My heart sank.

"Your mom was there," Stretch said. "I've never seen her so worried. She told me to take off. I thought I'd better track you down and let you know."

The signs were everywhere. I had to get to 7th Dimension headquarters at the University of Kansas to access the top-secret portal that could help me understand the transformation of Wade's consciousness.

But I had no way to get there. Even if I did, I had too much responsibility to leave town.

I rolled the window up, started the wagon, and hit the gas. I noticed Stretch yelling something at me as I drove past him, but I couldn't make it out, so I jammed on the brakes and rolled the window back down.

"*What?*"

"Did you know that dolphins have lips?"

31

I Never Had the Chance
to Say Goodbye

My mind was zipping around in a million different directions. I steered the station wagon onto Bird Parkway.
I needed to clear my head. I drove to the rec center, the one
place I knew I could go to do some deep thinking.

When Curtis, Stretch, and I were younger, we always
went to the rec center after school to play pickup basketball
until the sun went down. Now that the guys and I were
older and had the responsibilities that came with college,
jobs, and girlfriends, there was a lot less time for shooting
around together.

It was still early in the day, so it was quiet and there
weren't many kids in the building. I stopped by Mr. Shields's
office to say hey, but he wasn't there, so I picked up a basket-

ball from the rack in the hallway and wandered over to the court.

Having that ball in my hands helped to settle my nerves, but when I stepped to the free-throw line, I clanked my first half-dozen shots off the front of the rim. Coming up short was developing into a worrisome pattern.

"What was it that Wade used to tell you?" Mr. Shields's deep voice startled me. I hadn't heard him walk onto the court behind me, and I had no idea what he was talking about.

"Keep your chin up and stop moping?" I said.

"I suppose, but he also might have said, 'Knee, elbow, wrist—see the ball go through the hoop in your mind's eye before you release it.'"

That's exactly what Wade used to say whenever he was teaching me the nuts and bolts of free-throw shooting.

I took a couple of bounces to steady myself before visualizing the ball taking flight and slipping through the frayed nylon net. Then I bent my knees, raised my elbow, and flicked the ball toward the hoop.

Whoosh.

"That's better. Give me a dozen more just like it."

Mr. Shields rebounded for me as I buried the next twelve free throws in succession. The last one circled the rim a couple of times before giving way to proper form and gravity.

"When you stick with the fundamentals, it's easier to catch a break."

Mr. Shields hung around while I worked on my perimeter shooting. Even as the ball was dropping through the hole almost every time, Mr. Shields seemed to know I had a lot on my mind.

"This court is where I always go to figure stuff out," he said. "I suspect that's why you're here today."

Mr. Shields had been coaching for so long that reading his players' thoughts had become second nature. I spun the basketball on my index finger as I told him about everything that was weighing on me. I could feel the ball's pebbled, leathery surface grinding down the skin of my fingertip with every detail I offered.

Mr. Shields said he already knew about Curtis's surfing accident and Stretch's decision to quit the team and drop out of Jefferson. He hadn't heard about how poorly I thought I had played at tryouts the day before. He seemed surprised when I told him I was afraid Coach Kincaid might cut me.

"Curtis is tough. Stretch is resourceful. I suspect they're going to be okay," Mr. Shields said. He told me that coaches don't judge tryouts solely by how well someone plays. "We look for the intangibles, like attitude and potential. What seems like a setback can turn into an opportunity, if you view it in the right light."

I tucked the ball under my arm and told Mr. Shields about how challenging it was to work at Chip's Sporting Goods under Nathan, who always seemed agitated about something. Nathan was a regular at the rec center, so Mr. Shields was familiar with his tendency to go from annoyed to furious in nothing flat.

"Perhaps if you get to know Mister Freeman a little better, that wall might come down a bit. He's had to overcome obstacles in his life, the kind that most young folks never have to deal with."

I had been so busy trying to stay out of Nathan's crosshairs that I had never thought about what might be at the root of his anger. I made a mental note to look for an opportunity for a frank conversation with him, if for no other reason than because he was Lawrence's only friend other than me.

I decided to tell Mr. Shields about Rebecca's decision to leave Jefferson to enroll at the University of Kansas in the fall. It was happening at a time when the bond between us seemed to be growing stronger.

"I heard she was leaving the community college to pursue her passion, but I had no idea she was headed to KU. Sensing any irony there, Zeke?"

"It's hard to miss. Everyone's going to Kansas but me."

I doubted there was anyone within a twenty-mile radius of the rec center who hadn't heard that the University of Kansas had revoked my scholarship after I touched off a melee at the high school city finals. There was no use thinking about what might have been.

I told Mr. Shields I was concerned about Lawrence's mental state, but I didn't offer specific details about the conversation that took place at Lawrence's house. I didn't want to violate Lawrence's confidence, and I didn't think Mr. Shields would have believed me anyway.

"Lawrence is a gifted young fellow whose challenge is to harness all of that intuition and intelligence. With friends like you and Nathan, I'm certain he'll find his way."

Mr. Shields and I had covered quite a bit of ground. I was beginning to feel more in control of my life. I handed him the basketball.

"I guess that leaves the subject of my brother." There was no use in telling Mr. Shields about the eerie, dreamlike encounters I had recently had with Wade while running those fast breaks. He would have thought I had lost it. "There's such a huge hole in my life with Wade gone. I never had the chance to say goodbye."

Mr. Shields tugged on his white beard and smiled. He told me it was my choice to look at Wade in terms of the number of years he had been alive, but there were other ways to measure Wade's life. Then he gave me back the ball.

"This game is just one of his gifts to you, but it may well be the most meaningful. Think about how you apply the lessons Wade taught you on the court, how you respond to adversity and make choices that are grounded in integrity. Your brother might be gone, but he's still with you. Always will be."

32

I Was Just Leaving Anyway

After spending time with Mr. Shields, I realized that I had too many responsibilities in Los Angeles to drop every-thing and bolt for Kansas. His wise words carried me for the next couple of weeks as I fell into a routine of working at Chip's and spending precious time with Rebecca.

I was back to riding my bike everywhere after I put Cur-tis's Plymouth into cold storage in the carport next to Wade's pickup.

Coach Kincaid hadn't yet dropped the hammer on me, so I was attending basketball practice every day too. Curtis re-mained in a coma, Stretch spent his waking hours watching paint dry, Mom worked double shifts with regularity, and Lawrence was still barricaded in his bedroom.

It was my new normal.

"Stop daydreaming and get back to work, rookie."

If I had $1.98 for every time Nathan had said that to me, I would've had enough money to pay for car insurance by then.

Chip was holding his annual midsummer clearance sale, so the store was flooded with customers, and merchandise was flying off the shelves. I was hand-trucking a tall stack of cardboard boxes from the stock room when I turned a corner and crashed into someone.

"I was heading for the wellness section—now I *really* need to get there."

It was Rebecca. I had just mowed down my girlfriend. I pulled the cardboard heap off her and helped her to her feet.

Nathan heard the commotion and hurried over. "You all right, ma'am?"

"It's me, Nathan. Your employee is pretty clumsy, but I don't think he did it on purpose."

"As senior part-time trainee sales clerk, I have the option of suspending him without pay pending a full investigation," Nathan said.

"Nah. That'd just mean I'd have to pay for everything."

"Suit yourself."

I was surprised to see Rebecca at Chip's. It was the first time she had stopped by while I was at work. It was close enough to my break time, so I checked with Nathan to see if it would be okay to step away for a few minutes.

Nathan responded by rolling his eyes, which I took to mean I had his approval. Rebecca and I escaped to the break room. The fluorescent lights in there were cold and harsh.

"I'm leaving for Kansas."

"I know."

"No, I'm leaving today. Brock's driving me to the bus station in a couple of hours."

"What? I thought you were leaving at the end of summer."

Rebecca stared off into space for what felt like a half hour longer than eternity.

"I need to settle in and find work before the semester starts and all the good jobs are taken," she said finally. "I've applied for grants and student loans, but it's not enough to cover my tuition and expenses."

I wanted to ask Rebecca to delay her trip for a while so we could travel together, but I couldn't tell her the real reason why I needed to get to Kansas.

"Are you coming home for the holidays?" I asked. My heart was pounding with every emotion I could think of. If Rebecca were leaving sooner than planned, I wanted to know when I would see her again.

"Break's over, tenderfoot," Nathan said. "Don't make me write you up."

"No need for that, Nathan," Rebecca said. "I was just leaving anyway." Then she turned to me. "Walk me out, will you?"

Nathan's wrath, I decided, suddenly took second priority to an extra moment with Rebecca. When we got to the sidewalk, I reached to take her hand, but she pulled away.

"You don't need to decide right now if you'll be home for the holidays. Winter break is a long way off. You can just—"

"I don't think we should see each other anymore."

33

Here's Where It Gets Complicated

It took me a few seconds to process those words, because my ears were filled with the sound effects from every horror movie I had ever seen.

"Why shouldn't we see each other anymore?"

Rebecca seemed to anticipate my question and had a ready answer. "You've got so much going on right now—the team, this job, your friends. It's not fair to burden you with a long-distance relationship."

"Burden me?"

Being with Rebecca was way better than listening to Stretch's stupid jokes, and almost better than basketball.

Somewhere deep inside, I knew there had to be another reason.

I downshifted into desperation mode and forged on before she could respond. "It's only a few months till the holiday break. We can stay in touch by writing letters, and I'd even look after Brock until you got home and everything went back to normal."

Rebecca shifted her weight and didn't respond. It felt like a wall had gone up between us.

"Do you even *know* what insubordination is?" Nathan had deserted his post to confront me on the sidewalk.

"I think so." I had a rough idea, but I knew that Nathan would spell it out for me.

"It's when your boss asks you to do something, but you do something else instead. This isn't going to look good on your ninety-day performance evaluation."

Nathan's timing couldn't have been worse. How was I going to talk Rebecca out of breaking up with me while he was standing there quoting passages from the Chip's Sporting Goods employee handbook?

"It's all right, Nathan. I really am leaving now." Rebecca reached into her purse and dug out a crumpled envelope. She put it in my hand and walked away. Her echoing footsteps competed with the surrounding traffic until she turned the corner and disappeared.

I stuffed the envelope into my back pocket.

"Chip must've slipped her your final paycheck when I wasn't looking."

"Shut up, Nathan."

Nathan and I went back to work. We didn't say another word to each other for the rest of my shift. I clocked out and went to the break room to pull my backpack from my locker. Basketball practice was a couple of hours away, so I bought a root beer from the soft drink machine and settled in to read Rebecca's letter.

I caught a vague whiff of her perfume when I broke the seal on the envelope. I took a swig of root beer and grimaced, the same way Humphrey Bogart does in the movie *Casablanca* when he throws down a shot of whisky, tortured by the woman he loves but can never have.

Rebecca's handwriting was pretty. I had a feeling her words wouldn't be.

Dear Ezekiel:

This is a difficult letter for me to write, but it's a lot easier than saying this stuff to you in person. For starters, I've been haunted by what happened to Curtis. I wish I could have done more for him.

Done more? She restarted his heart and got him breathing again after he had drowned under a wall of seawater.

I didn't know enough about how to perform CPR. If I did, I think I could have gotten Curtis breathing a lot earlier, and he probably wouldn't be in a coma right now.

Anyway, I need to get to the University of Kansas right away so I can get ready for the start of the semester. There is so much to learn.

Rebecca was breaking up with me to get a head start on

her classes. I had a sense there was a lot more going on than that.

There's more. You weren't my first boyfriend, but I learned so much from you, and not just about basketball. Watching you learn the hard way about the importance of making good decisions caused me to take a long look at my life. I chose to commit to you, but I now know I wasn't ready to do that. I'm sorry if I hurt you. I never meant to.

Too late.

There's one more thing, and here's where it gets complicated. All my life, guys have walked out on me. First my dad when I was really young. That left me with my numbskull stepbrother Brock as my shining example of how men are supposed to behave around women, and we both know how that's worked out so far.

There have been others—coaches, counselors, a couple of boyfriends, boys who were friends. One after another, they were here one day and gone the next. One of my therapists once told me I had a fear of abandonment, and that was before he left too.

I've always relied on others who eventually let me down. Someplace deep inside, it feels safer to say goodbye before you have the chance to leave me too.

I was doing my best to understand that last part, but it

only made me feel sorry for Rebecca, which was the last thing
I think she would've wanted me to do.

> *You deserve to be with someone who has way fewer
> problems than I do. I'm grateful for the time we spent to-
> gether, and I know you will have a great life.*
> *Love always,*
> *Rebecca*

34

It's Complicated

Rebecca was my first-ever girlfriend. Even so, I knew enough about women by then to understand that when one tells you to have a nice life, the translation is: she's not planning for you to be part of hers.

I was surprised to see Nathan strutting back into the break room. I thought his shift had ended with mine, but he told me Chip had granted him full-time status for the rest of the summer, as well as a title change to assistant supervisor.

"There's no substitute for experience," Nathan said.

Nathan snagged his backpack from his locker, opened a soft drink, and saddled up on the opposite end of the lunch table. I saw him pull out two plastic bags containing the mystery food he was famous for—tiny chunks of bread baked into the shape of chess pieces.

Then he removed a folded-up sheet of paper from his backpack and spread it out on the lunch table. There were sixty-four black and white squares on it.

It was a chessboard.

Nathan dumped the contents of one of the bags onto the board—eight pawns, two rooks, two knights, two bishops, a queen, and a king. It was a full set. He lined up the pieces on one side of the board and then repeated the process on the other. I could tell the sets apart because the second one was sprinkled with powdered sugar.

Nathan caught me staring at him. It seemed to rankle him. "Find something else to do, hayseed."

I was already doing something else—busy feeling sorry for myself before Nathan had sat down for what appeared to be a chess match versus the Invisible Man.

"It's a free country," was all I could come up with.

Nathan ignored me. He sized up the chessboard for several minutes as he sipped from his can. Then he pushed forward a pawn. He made a countermove on the opposite side of the board, then another.

And it was on.

The furious, back-and-forth action continued until a sugar-crusted bishop captured an unsweetened knight. But instead of slamming the unlucky horse onto the table next to the game board, as I had seen chess masters do on TV, Nathan popped the doomed piece into his mouth.

When there were only a few pieces left, he slid a queen diagonally across the board and mumbled a word that sounded vaguely like "Checkmate," but it was hard to tell because he had so much bread in his mouth when he said it.

Nathan rounded up the uneaten pieces and returned them to their pouches. "Snack for later," he said before polishing off his soda and tossing the can into the recycling container.

"Who won?"

"Is that supposed to be funny?"

"Just trying to make friendly conversation," I said.

There was no use hanging around where I wasn't wanted. I gathered up my stuff and headed for the break room exit. I got as far as the doorway.

"Chess and basketball have a lot in common."

That peace offering was the last thing I expected from Nathan. I checked to make sure he wasn't flashing a weapon before going back to my original spot at the far end of the table.

"Like what?" I had never thought about the parallels that could be drawn, but Nathan had.

"We both look into our opponent's eyes to size up their strengths, expose their weaknesses. We look for patterns, hunt down gaps in defense, make decisions based on probable outcomes. We attack, retreat, then attack again. It's a ballet of the mind."

"Anything else?"

"Yeah. Winning is the relief I feel from not losing."

Deep stuff. I sensed a breakthrough in our working relationship. To keep the conversation going, I asked about the time he had thrown in the towel at the junior college state chess championship last semester.

"How come you walked away from that title match?"

"No reason."

Not possible. People had a reason for everything they did. And Nathan was a very determined person, to say the least.

I had witnessed that grueling, ill-fated match in person, on an assignment to write a story for the school paper. After it ended, Nathan declined my request for a postgame interview. That left me to speculate on why he had surrendered, so I theorized in my story that he might have taken ill and been unable to continue.

Nathan hadn't yet exited the break room, so I probed deeper. "When someone says, 'No reason,' it usually means there *is* a reason, but they don't want to talk about it."

"Get out of my face." Nathan threw the wall back up just as quickly as he had lowered it.

With nothing left to say, I retreated. I made it a little farther that second time, all the way to the time clock outside Chip's office, when I heard Nathan shouting something.

"It's complicated!" Nathan said.

I stepped back in and glanced up at the wall clock. Basketball practice was ninety minutes away. "I've got some time. Why don't you break it down for me?"

I took my original seat. Nathan shot me the death stare long enough for me to wonder whether I should have kept walking. The hum coming from the soft drink machine was the only sound in the break room.

I sat and watched as Nathan consumed the rest of his chess pieces. Then he broke his silence, and the floodgates opened.

35

Game Over

Nathan explained that the scouting report on Jefferson's Northern California rivals had revealed that they were skilled and experienced, but their emotions tended to run high.

"Coach told us we'd have an advantage if we applied variations to our normal approach in the middle game, forcing tactical actions known as combinations in situations where our sacrifices could result in tangible gains," Nathan said. "The strategy was designed to frustrate and wear down our opponents, and hopefully it would lead to mental lapses in the endgame."

Nathan said the plan had worked over several matches, but midway through the tournament, the other team caught wind of Jefferson's ploy and set retaliatory countermeasures into motion. The team score was tied by the time Nathan settled into a chair for the final match that would determine the state championship.

I remembered writing in my story that Nathan's game development was clever and calculated as he worked to gain control of the center while focusing on king safety and pawn structure. But by the time the match had transitioned deeply into the middle game, Nathan and his opponent were locked in a fierce battle, dead even.

Then without warning, Nathan stood up, pulled a crinkled, white handkerchief from his pocket, and tossed it onto the table. The crowd gasped as he walked out of the building and into the cold night air. I ran out to interview him for my story, but he told me I should talk to the player who had won, because it would make for a more interesting game recap.

I thought that enough time had elapsed between that ill-fated chess tournament and our summer jobs at Chip's, so I asked Nathan one more time to level with me about his decision to concede the match. "Why don't you just give it to me straight?" I said.

Nathan instinctively reached for a baked chess piece, only to find he had already consumed the contents of both bags. A familiar anger washed over his face.

"It's kind of quiet in here. Is everything okay?" Chip Spears had poked his head through the break room doorway, no doubt to make sure there were no fisticuffs.

I remembered Mr. Shields's advice. "We're good, Chip. Nathan and I were just getting to know each other a little better." I was hoping Mr. Shields was right about exploring the inner Nathan.

Chip went back to his office.

Nathan stared at his empty plastic bags. "Chess isn't about winning," he said.

I was growing frustrated by Nathan's evasive answers. Wasn't winning as important in chess as it was in basketball? "Help me out. What does that mean?"

Nathan said his parents were killed in a car accident while bringing him home from the hospital when he was just a few days old.

That news sent a shiver rolling down my spine.

He said the local newspaper reported that a drunk driver had drifted over the center divider and slammed head-on into their vehicle. Nathan was gravely injured, but he survived and was taken in and raised by his grandparents.

"Poppa worked as an auto mechanic, but he spent nights and weekends hustling on LA's underground chess gambling circuit to make ends meet," Nathan said. "He drifted between auto repair garages and city parks, taking on challengers in high-stakes games. He was known as the Grease Monkey Grandmaster. Taught me everything I know."

Nathan said his grandfather looked at chess the same way I approached basketball—through cautious observation, by looking into the future and considering the consequences of one's actions.

"Poppa showed me how to think logically and trust my intuition," Nathan said.

But something seemed off. Nathan kept referring to his grandfather in the past tense. I asked him about it.

"Are you sure you want to know, rookie?"

My question had struck a nerve. "Yeah, I guess."

If Nathan had tucked away a secret edible chess piece for emergencies, he would've busted it out right then.

"I was about nine when Poppa got into a match with a high roller named Gus, a club player with a rep for losing his temper when things weren't falling his way."

Gee, that reminded me of someone.

Nathan said his grandfather was running late for dinner, so he went for a speedy victory with a chess gambit known as the Fishing Pole Trap.

"Poppa baited Gus into chasing his knight all over the board. When Gus finally captured that knight, he was totally exposed. Poppa took one of Gus's pawns with one of his own, then slid that pawn and his queen into position. It was checkmate. Game over."

After that, it was game over for Poppa. Nathan said Gus pulled out a gun and shot his grandfather dead, right there on the park bench.

36

I Thought I Must Be
Seeing Things

We sat there and stared at each other for about a month. Neither one of us said anything after Nathan dropped that bomb in the break room.

Finally, he cut through the silence by saying that the details of his grandfather's death had all come out during the trial, including why Gus pulled the trigger. "He said he was really angry with Poppa for disrespecting him. Anything else you wanna know?"

Nathan's description of the circumstances leading to his grandfather's senseless murder helped me to understand Nathan better. I felt bad about making him bring up painful memories, so I tried to change the subject.

"What about the bread chessmen?"

"After Gus was convicted and sentenced to life in prison, I told Grammy I was quitting chess. I couldn't deal with how a game I loved so much could cause me so much pain."

Nathan said his grandmother worked in a bakery. One day not long after he walked away from chess, she arrived home from work toting a sack of baked goods.

"From a distance, they looked like lumpy pretzels. When she offered me one at the dinner table, I shoved it away." He said that upon closer inspection, he realized it was a baked pawn. "Grammy said it was a special recipe and told me to eat one every time I felt the anger building up inside."

Nathan said his grandmother claimed to use an ancestral baking formula, handed down by generations of chefs and pastry makers in her family. All she would tell him about the ingredients was that they included joyful flour and thankful starter yeast.

"I knew it was all a bunch of hocus-pocus, but I took them to chess matches anyway. Now I eat one on every capture. It really pisses off my opponents. Are we done here? I've got to get back to work."

Nathan seemed to be in a better place after our conversation, but I still didn't know why he had conceded the pivotal match in the state finals. I asked him again as he was getting ready to leave.

"The kid needed that match a lot more than I did."

Nathan seemed to allude to his desire to save his opponent from the anguish of a devastating loss. For a fleeting moment, it reminded me of my own decision to take the last shot in the regional title game rather than pass the ball to Brock. Still, it felt like Nathan was giving me the brush-off. "How could you possibly know what your opponent was thinking? It's okay if you don't want to tell me."

"Just a hunch," he said. "Don't you ever get those on the basketball court?"

Sure, but I didn't see the connection. I had developed my ability to read opposing players based on their movements on the court. In a chess match, all Nathan could do was sit there and stare down his opponent. It was different.

Or so I thought.

"I had a feeling that if I beat that kid, it would've scarred him for life. I wasn't interested in going there, not after what I've been through."

"What about your friends on the chess team?" I knew that Nathan's teammates had been counting on him to come through. When I interviewed his teammates after the match, I found that they were bitter about the outcome.

"If they'd played better in the tournament, I wouldn't have been in that position. I made my best call."

Nathan left the break room and punched back in. The clock on the wall said basketball practice was more than an hour away, but I thought it was best to get on my bike and ride to Jefferson to warm up. I retrieved my backpack and ball from my locker and waved goodbye to Chip on my way out the door.

As I was unlocking my bike, I noticed some people who appeared to be homeless milling around the parking lot. I felt a tap on my shoulder. I whirled around and was standing face-to-face with the mystery drop-kick kid.

"Hello, butt."

"You scared the crap out of me!"

"Mae'n ddrwg gen i."

"What?"

"It means *I'm sorry* in Welsh. I didn't mean to scare you that way."

I remembered Rebecca saying at the memorial service that the mystery teenager had used a Welsh expression when he called me "butt," which would explain why I was having a hard time understanding him. I noticed he was wearing the same odd clothing he had on at Wade's funeral.

"Why are you following me?"

"Long story there, butt. Involves a rugby ball and a bit of a scuffle."

I was about to ask the kid for more details, but our conversation was interrupted by a guy in a pickup truck honking his horn on the other side of the Chip's Sporting Goods parking lot.

I tried to ignore it, but the man was persistent. He kept honking as if he were trying to get my attention. Then the driver pushed opened the door and stepped out onto the blacktop.

"Zeke!"

What in the world? I thought I must be seeing things. It was my father. What was he doing in Los Angeles?

I noticed someone sitting on the passenger side. I squinted my eyes to get a better look. It was Lawrence. He was chewing a wad of gum at high speed. Lawrence blew a giant bubble. When it exploded, I could hear the sound from the opposite end of the parking lot.

When I turned back to face the kid, he was gone.

37

You Must Agree to Take Me with You

I rode my bike across the parking lot and leaned it against the pickup truck. My father walked over and extended his hand, which was weird, because I was expecting a hug.

I thought about showing off my new, Chip Spears–approved handshake, but I changed my mind, ignoring Dad's outstretched hand and hugging him instead. His army jacket was covered in coffee stains and reeked of cigarette smoke.

I looked over my dad's shoulder toward Lawrence, who popped another wedge of bubblegum into his mouth but did not make eye contact.

My dad's eyes, on the other hand, were bloodshot. His gray hair was pointing in all directions at once. He smiled as if to convey that he was okay, but he looked weary and exhausted, as if he had been driving for countless hours, which was likely the case, since his home in Denver was a thousand miles away.

I led my father a good distance away from Lawrence and the truck. I had a lot of questions for him. I started with the basics. "What are you doing here? Is everything all right? Why is Lawrence in the truck?"

My dad rubbed his hand across several days' worth of beard growth. "Your friend over there sent me a letter. He said you were in trouble and needed my help."

That was weird. I wasn't in any more trouble than usual.

I only had a best friend in a coma, another one who had just quit our basketball team and dropped out of college, and a girlfriend who had broken up with me minutes earlier and was getting ready to move halfway across the country.

"He sent you a letter?"

My dad reached into his jacket pocket and pulled out a rumpled envelope.

"Here."

I glanced back at Lawrence. There was a lot of gum chewing going on, but not much else.

"Why didn't you call me?"

"It's all in there."

I unfolded the letter. Lawrence must have memorized Dad's address from our road trip the previous year, when we stopped in Denver on our way to the University of Kansas.

There was no question about the letter's authenticity. It was written in pencil, and I recognized that precision handwriting, words leaning slightly forward, to the right, like Law-

rence in his chair in math class back in high school when he
would raise his hand to correct Mr. Appleton.

> Dear Mr. Archer:
> My name is Sherman Tuckerman. Both of
> my friends call me Lawrence. It's kind of
> a nickname, but that's a long story for
> another time. You can call me Lawrence,
> though, unless you're more comfortable calling
> me Sherman, which would also be okay.

That was quite a thorough introduction by Lawrence. As
usual, he was leaving nothing to chance.

> I'm writing this letter from my bedroom,
> where I do most of my critical thinking,
> unless I'm in the school library at McDerney
> Continuation, where I write letters to
> scientists and mathematicians about my
> theories on space travel.

I checked my watch. If Lawrence's intro went on much
longer, I would run the risk of being late for practice.

> I'm writing to tell you that Zeke is in
> trouble and needs your help.

Finally.

Zeke needs to get to the University of Kansas to speak with a certain someone about a certain something that might or might not have something to do with advanced biomathematics, or basketball's top-secret portal to a certain interdimensional energy being, or dolphins carrying telepathic messages to a certain surfer, or Zeke's one and only chance to unravel the mystery of Wade's eternal consciousness.

Whoa.

I'm sorry to have to be so mysterious about certain details, but I'm bound by a vow of secrecy to forces greater than me. Don't worry, though. If I seem strange to you, it's okay, because I'm normal to myself.

I was glad Lawrence had tossed in those disclaimers. That way, he would save my dad the trouble of having to ask questions for which there were no credible answers.

Zeke got a job at Chip's Sporting Goods to earn money to pay for a trip to Kansas. Zeke's boss, by the way, is my other friend, Nathan Freeman, who plays chess, bosses Zeke around, and gets angry all the time.

Anyway, earlier today I intercepted a

highly confidential communiqué saying that the window of opportunity for Zeke to meet with that certain someone would soon be closing. Once that happens, Zeke's opportunity to gain vital knowledge about Wade's fate will be lost forever.

I decided to ask for your help. Zeke needs you to drive him to a certain Entity headquarters adjacent to Allen Fieldhouse. But there is one condition.

Uh-oh, here it comes.

You must agree to take me with you, because you'll need me to run the mathematical calculations on the road, and Zeke will need me to clear the path for him.

I might or might not have already received permission from my dad to go. My address is on the back of the envelope. I've already packed my aluminum lunchbox with enough freeze-dried training food and bubblegum to survive the journey.

I'll be waiting patiently here in my bedroom for you to swing by and pick me up.

Sincerely yours,

Sherman "Lawrence" Tuckerman

Future Mars Astronaut-in-Training

Los Angeles, California

38

That's Going to Leave a Mark

I glared at Lawrence from across the parking lot and shook my head in disbelief. If he saw me, he didn't acknowledge it.

I stuffed Lawrence's letter back into its envelope and returned it to my father. I was concerned because he had accepted Lawrence's absurd plan and driven straight to Los Angeles without checking with me first. Maybe my dad was more nuts than I had realized.

"You drove all the way here nonstop from Denver based on that letter?"

"I've spoken to your mother. It seemed like she was doing better."

Either my dad hadn't heard my question, or he had ignored it. "I guess. She doesn't cry as much these days."

Dad pulled a pack of cigarettes from his coat pocket. He slid one out and lit it.

"You know those things are going to kill you."

"Lawrence is your friend, right?"

It was the second time in as many questions that my dad had changed the subject. I remembered how he used to do that whenever he got into a screaming match with my mom after Wade took off for boot camp.

"Yeah, Dad, but he's kind of different. He's got a vivid imagination."

"Has he ever lied to you?"

"I guess not."

Technically, that was true. But there had been a bazillion times since Lawrence and I had met when I had needed to give Lawrence's concept of reality plenty of breathing room. I knew my dad was trying to make a point, but to what end, I didn't know.

"So that's a no?"

"Uh-huh."

Dad took an extra-long drag from his cigarette and exhaled a massive cloud of smoke. He flicked the half-used butt onto the ground and snuffed it out with his combat boot.

"I retired from the army a few months ago. Gotta lotta time on my hands these days."

I wasn't sure that was a legitimate reason for my dad to drive halfway across the country. It also felt weird for him to be pushing his way back into my life after he had divorced my mom and vanished several years ago.

"It was nice of you to come all the way here, but I've got too much going on right now to go to Kansas."

My dad smiled. I could tell he was disappointed. He put his hand on my shoulder and locked his weary eyes onto mine.

"I understand," he said. "Maybe next time."

Lawrence caught my attention from the truck cab. I could see he was holding a sheet of paper. Now what?

I knew my best chance to access the 7th Dimension's top-secret portal to learn Wade's destiny wouldn't come from dragging Brock Decker and Jed Swagerty down the court with me on some random, perfectly executed fast break.

I needed to return to Entity headquarters. That meant traveling to eastern Kansas, to the grove of trees adjacent to Allen Fieldhouse, to confront the fake janitor, the man otherwise known as Dr. James Naismith.

I was torn. I didn't know what to do.

"I have a lot of responsibilities, Dad. I've got a job, and I'm trying to make the team at Jefferson. Plus, I don't even know if Mom would let me go." At least I no longer had a girlfriend to factor into the equation. Otherwise, I would've chucked that onto the list too.

The shrill sound of the truck's blaring horn sucker-punched my eardrums. I turned to find Lawrence's arm sticking out the window. In his hand was a folded-up sheet of paper fluttering in the summer breeze.

"You could have gotten out of the truck and just handed it to me!"

There was no response from Lawrence, which I had come to understand was a kind of response that didn't require a counterresponse. I walked over, snatched the note from his hand, and unfolded it.

Last week I intercepted another 7th Dimension communiqué. It said Dr. Naismith will soon depart Entity headquarters at the University of Kansas. When he does, his knowledge about the transformation of Wade's consciousness will depart with him. Dr. Naismith won't return to Earth in our lifetime. We don't have much time.

What did he mean by *we*?

My dad yelled to me from across the parking lot. "What does the note say?"

I motioned with my hand to let him know I had everything under control.

I looked at Lawrence in disbelief, searching for a clue as to whether what he was saying in that note was real. Lawrence detonated a massive bubble that sprayed pink shrapnel onto the inside of Dad's windshield. Then the pencil emperor scribbled out another note and handed it to me through the window.

That's going to leave a mark.

I felt my shoulders squeezing the base of my neck. I was scared and frazzled. "How much time do we have?"

"Dr. Naismith departs Earth twenty-four hours from now." Lawrence had actually spoken his words out loud that time.

"How long will it take us to drive to Allen Fieldhouse?"

"Going the speed limit? Twenty-four hours. The longer we delay, the faster your dad needs to drive."

39

My Hands Got Sweaty
All Over Again

Lawrence finally convinced me. I had to drop everything and go to Kansas.

But I also had to let the people know who were counting on me. I walked past my dad and back inside to ask Chip if I could take a leave of absence right in the middle of the annual summer sale, the store's busiest time of the year.

Nathan was ringing up a customer at the cash register when I tried to slip past him on my way to Chip's office.

No such luck. Nathan saw me and scowled. He seemed to know something was up.

Chip's office door was open. I knocked to announce my arrival.

"I thought you already left. Is something wrong?"

I wasn't sure how Chip knew it was me, because he never looked up from the papers he was shuffling.

"Everything's fine, Chip. I just need to ask you something." I was a nervous wreck. The palms of my hands were sweaty.

Chip got up from his desk and extended his hand. It all happened so fast, there was no time to discreetly wipe mine on my pant leg. I attempted to distract him by squeezing his hand with the iron grip of death. I looked him in the eye and grinned with all the sincerity of an esteemed colleague. Three pumps. Three seconds. Release.

Chip flexed his hand a couple of times to get the circulation moving again. Then he wiped it on his polo shirt and told me to take a seat.

"What's up?"

"Nothing. I just need to ask if I can take a few days off, maybe a week. I need to go to Kansas to take care of some stuff."

Chip tilted his chin downward and frowned. I could tell he was disappointed. "We're kind of busy around here right now. When do you need to go?"

"I was thinking about leaving now."

Chip took a moment to let the news sink in before continuing his paper shuffle. He emerged with what looked like my employment application. "You've been here, what, two weeks?"

"Yes, sir."

"And you're asking to take a leave of absence?"

"Yes, sir, I guess so."

Chip got up and pulled a bound copy of the Chip's Sporting Goods employee handbook from his bookshelf. I gulped as he thumbed through it until he stopped on a page somewhere in the middle.

"Says here you need to clear your ninety-day probationary period *before* you can request a leave of absence. If my math serves me correctly, you haven't met that requirement."

"Yes, sir. I guess not."

Chip had me on the ropes. I needed the job, but I needed to get to Kansas more.

He put on his reading glasses and read the policy again to himself, his lips moving in cadence with the rules written to protect his business. The only sound in his office was coming from the wall clock as it ticked away precious seconds.

With Chip deep in thought, the image of my brother popped into my head out of nowhere. It caused me to recall the time years ago at a theme park when I had my heart set on climbing aboard a roller coaster that I had no business attempting to conquer. I wasn't tall enough, according to the rules posted at the ride's entrance, so Wade asked the attendant if he would allow me to get on the ride just that one time.

I decided to go for it.

"I don't suppose you could make an exception?" I said, the pitch of my voice rising.

I didn't have to wait long for Chip's decision. It came swiftly and without emotion. "I've got a business to run. If I made an exception for you, I'd have to make one for everybody."

I didn't have to think about my next move, because Chip made it for me.

"I'm terminating your employment for cause—violation of company policy."

I had never heard that phrase before. I stiffened my posture. "Sir?"

"I'll translate—it means you're fired. Turn in your polo shirt and clean out your locker."

My hands got sweaty all over again. I had never been fired before, which made sense, because the job at Chip's was my first ever.

I responded with panic in my voice. "Am I banned from the store for life?"

I could tell that Chip was doing his level best to muzzle a grin. "That would only happen if you were let go for gross misconduct. You're still welcome here as a customer."

I felt a wave of relief glide across my stomach as I got up and headed for the exit.

"One more thing," Chip said. "Do me a favor and let Nathan know on your way out."

Great. I had been hoping to avoid Nathan's wrath. No such luck. Even though I was off the clock, I considered it an order from Chip.

"Will do, boss."

I made my way across the store and found Nathan at the checkout counter ringing up a customer. He handed the woman a package and her receipt. "Thank you for shopping at Chip's. Have a nice day."

When Nathan saw me, he seemed to know that bad news awaited.

"I just quit. Family reasons."

Nathan's nostrils flared. He slammed the cash register drawer.

I apologized for ruining his summer and walked out the door. When I got to the pickup truck, I motioned for Lawrence to get in the back seat of the crew cab.

"No way," he said. "I called shotgun. Remember?"

40

I Sat and Wondered Where My Life Was Going

I loaded my bike into the truck bed, lobbed my backpack and ball onto the back seat, and climbed in. My father pulled out of Chip's parking lot and into heavy LA traffic.

"We've got to make a stop," I said from the back seat.

"You'll have to speak up. We can't hear you up here." It was a rare note of humor from Lawrence. I noticed my dad crack a smile through the rearview mirror. I wasn't in the mood, but I appreciated the effort.

"Take Chamberlain Drive to the college!" I shouted.

I needed to speak with Coach Kincaid before we hit the open road. Leaving town without advance notice wouldn't go over well with him. He hadn't made his final roster cuts, so I knew I would be experiencing the season from the bleachers if I just disappeared.

When Dad drove up to the gym, I saw the Puckett Painting van illegally parked in front of the double-door entrance. I wondered whether Mr. Puckett and Stretch were now doing touch-up work after they had finished painting the arena's interior a few weeks earlier.

"I'll be back in a couple of minutes."

When I walked inside, I saw Stretch in the gym, but not his father. Stretch was dressed in his usual cap and paint-stained coveralls, but he didn't have a paintbrush in his hand.

He had a basketball.

Stretch took a couple of dribbles and buried a fallaway from inside the paint.

"Don't get your hopes up," he said. "Coach lets me shoot around on my lunch hour. I'm trying to stay in shape." Stretch tossed me the ball with a crisp, two-handed chest pass. "Here, take a couple."

I returned the ball with a soft bounce pass. "Can't, I'm leaving town."

"Brock threaten you again?"

"Lawrence and my dad are outside waiting for me. No time to explain. Where's Coach?"

Stretch's jaw unhinged itself and drooped below his geeky neck. "In the office," he said.

I took off for Coach Kincaid's office at the other end of Jefferson's athletic complex.

I had just made it to the gym's rear door when Stretch's shrill voice echoed across the building. "I went to check on Curtis before work!"

"How is he?"

"Still in intensive care. They wouldn't let me see him. I'm not family, like you."

"Try again. Say you're my cousin," I said as I waved good-bye and kept moving, remembering what Lawrence had said about the 7th Dimension's deadline. I didn't want my father driving the sixteen hundred miles to Allen Fieldhouse at an unsafe speed.

Coach Kincaid's office door was open. I walked in.

"Oh, good, you're here. I need to talk to you about the fast break. I want you to think about—"

"Coach, I need to leave town in a hurry. I'm not sure when I'll be back."

My words transformed Coach Kincaid's warm smile into an expression of concern. "Is everything all right?"

"It's a long story." And if I told it to him, he would think I had lost my mind.

Coach Kincaid stood up from his desk and flipped through a three-ring binder. It reminded me of moments earlier when Chip Spears had gone in search of documents that sealed my fate as a former store employee.

"Here it is." Coach pulled a sheet of paper from his notebook. It looked like a list of players trying out for the team. "I'm making final roster decisions after practice today. If you're not here, I'm afraid you're not going to make the squad."

"Yes, sir."

I had learned to answer that way from having a father and brother who had both served in the military. It was a way to be polite and show respect without revealing anything, like the pangs of regret bombarding my stomach.

For a split second, I wasn't sure I had made the right decision. Being on that basketball team was the most important thing in my life, even if Curtis and Stretch couldn't join me. But I had already decided to seek out my brother's ultimate fate. There was no turning back.

"Best of luck, Zeke. I hope we'll see you during the season. We could use your support."

I shook Coach's hand as I left, not bothering to trot out Chip's professional version of the handshake. I guess I thought it didn't matter anymore. By the time I made my way back to the gym, Stretch was gone.

I opened the door to the crew cab's rear seat and climbed back inside.

"How'd it go with the coach?" my dad said.

"Let's just go." I turned my head to the side to make sure he didn't see my tears.

My dad pulled onto Chamberlain Drive and headed toward Interstate 10. Lawrence put himself in the proper headspace for a lengthy road trip by popping three wedges of bubblegum into his mouth in rapid succession. I sat and wondered where my life was going.

Dad pulled over to the curb just short of the eastbound freeway on-ramp and brought the truck to a stop. "Shouldn't you tell your mother we're hitting the road?" he said.

"You said you spoke to her. You said you thought she was doing better."

"That was about a week after the funeral."

41

You've Got Two Minutes, Mr. Short, Then I'm Calling Security

I couldn't believe my dad hadn't called my mom to at least give her a courtesy heads-up that he was thinking of taking me and Lawrence halfway across the country in search of lord knows what. It felt like my life was unraveling before my eyes.

The first time I could remember feeling anger toward my father was when my mother told me he had moved out and left town without saying goodbye. I couldn't tell him how pissed off I was at the time, because I had no way of reaching him. After a while, my anger turned to bitterness and resentment.

Enough years had passed for my feelings to have softened by the time my dad showed up unannounced in Chip's parking lot.

"I don't suppose you got permission from Lawrence's father to take him with us."

There was a long silence inside the truck. The force of cars whizzing past us buffeted the windows and shook our vehicle. Lawrence and my dad looked straight ahead. Neither moved a muscle. It occurred to me that this was what it must be like when Nathan contemplated his next move in a heated chess match—anger versus silence, each staring the other down across an innocent chessboard.

Lawrence was first to flinch. "Our fathers spoke to each other at my house. Mine said he wanted to go with us. I almost had to slap him to get him to stay behind and guard my bedroom."

That would've been funny if I hadn't realized that Lawrence was serious.

My father cracked his window and lit another cigarette before steering the truck back onto the road. He drove past the freeway on-ramp and made a U-turn. I didn't have to ask where we were going. I already knew.

We made it to Mikan Memorial Hospital in a matter of minutes. "Wait here," was all I said as I slammed the truck door behind me.

I marched into the hospital lobby and was greeted by the same security guard who had been there the last time. He must have recognized me in the parking lot, because he was

holding up my visitor's badge as I approached the information desk.

"Welcome back, Mr. Short. Third floor. You'll need this."

I clipped the badge to my shirt and double-timed it across
the lobby.

Either the security guard was very good at his job, or he
didn't like me. Most likely both, because when the elevator
doors opened, out stepped my mother. She wore a look of
panic on her face.

"Honey, what's wrong?"

"Everything's fine. I just dropped by to let you know I'm
going away for a few days."

My mom threw her hands up in the air. "I don't have
time for this, Zeke. I've got a whole hospital ward full of
problems."

For as long as I could remember, my mom was at her best
when organizing trouble by making it bend to her will. My
going-away-for-a-few-days thing was just another detail in a
busy day full of them. It was as if she were telling me and my
unscheduled travel plans to take a number at the reception
desk.

I didn't have much time either, so I went for the direct
approach.

"I've had a crappy day. Rebecca dumped me. Chip fired
me. Coach cut me. I'm going to KU to take care of some stuff.
Lawrence is waiting for me outside in the truck."

"Wade's truck?"

"No. Dad's."

Mom punched the elevator button. A few seconds later, the door opened, and she pulled me inside.

"Three, please," she said to the orderly standing in front of the control panel.

An antiseptic odor and stark fluorescent lighting overcame my senses when the doors opened. Mom hustled me over to a vacant nurse's station for a conversation I didn't want to have and had no time for anyway.

"You never gave me the full story of why you went to Kansas the last time. Now you're doing it again?"

"Yes, ma'am."

When my mom asked me how I had managed to lose my job and my roster spot on the same day, I just shrugged my shoulders. I couldn't tell her the reason why.

"What about Rebecca?"

That one was tougher to answer, because I was still trying to figure it out. "Said she needed to break up with me before I broke up with her, or something."

Mom looked up at the wall clock and wrinkled her forehead. She picked up a clipboard from the desk and made some notes on a patient's chart.

"What about Lawrence? How's his state of mind?"

"Sherman Tuckerman is in the zone."

I waited for her to ask how my father was doing, but she never did. I figured she already knew.

Our conversation was interrupted by the sound of a horn and a voice on the PA system.

"Code Blue!"

I knew from having a nurse for a mom that Code Blue meant a patient was in the throes of a medical emergency that likely wouldn't end well.

My mom sprung to her feet. "Just go. There's nothing I can do. I've got too much going on around here."

I managed to get in a question of my own as she grabbed up medical supplies from a cabinet.

"How's Curtis?"

"Still in a coma," she said, pointing toward the door leading to the ICU. "You've got two minutes, Mr. Short, then I'm calling security."

I pulled open the door to the ICU and walked inside as my mom took off in the opposite direction. I found the familiar paper sign reminding me that I had to be immediate family in order to be standing there reading it.

Curtis's bronze suntan was gone. His chalky, ghostlike complexion made it seem as if he had crawled inside a flour sack and fallen asleep before I arrived. He was still hooked up to machines that were monitoring his lack of progress.

I touched his hand. Cold and lifeless. It didn't make sense that a person who loved the ocean so much could nearly drown in it. I felt helpless and scared.

To this day, I don't know why I did it, but I squeezed my eyes shut and visualized what I thought Huey the Surf God might look like.

I didn't have a lot to go on. I put him in a pair of board shorts with a surfboard tucked under his arm. It wasn't the modern type of board crafted from polyurethane foam and covered with layers of fiberglass cloth. In my mind's eye, I saw

Huey toting a longboard, a fifteen-footer made of Hawaiian koa wood, without fins or a leash. Old school.

Huey was on dawn patrol, wading through ankle-deep tide toward the waiting swell, his sparkling eyes fixed in a weightless gaze on the pink horizon ahead.

I licked my lips, concentrated with all my brain power, and made a simple request on behalf of my best friend, Curtis Short.

I asked Huey the Surf God for an exception.

42

I Went Back to the Cold Case and Got Another Cheese Sandwich

I opened my eyes, hoping for a miracle. I stared at Curtis and searched for any sign that Huey the Surf God had pulled some strings, or cut through the red tape, or did what you hope specialty gods do when someone files a sincere request for assistance.

Nothing.

I felt my ears giving off heat out of embarrassment, but that was it. It seemed silly to have even tried. I sensed that Mom's two-minute time limit was up, so I assured an unconscious Curtis that his station wagon was safely stashed at my apartment, and I said goodbye.

As I turned to walk away, the fluorescent light above Curtis's gurney flickered, sending a rush of adrenaline through my body that gave me the willies. I looked at Curtis one final time, but the only change I noticed was my own greater understanding of what false hope felt like.

I left the hospital and climbed back into my dad's truck.

"Can I drive?" Lawrence, all of fifteen years old, seemed serious.

"No." So was my dad.

"Suit yourself. Punch it." No doubt Lawrence had been watching too many late-night TV movies in which the bad guys attempt to outrun and outfox the cops.

I cinched my seatbelt as my dad piloted the truck toward Interstate 10. After a few blocks, I saw the drop-kick kid, William Webb Ellis, standing on the street corner with his thumb out.

Clearly, I was losing my sanity.

"Did you see that guy hitchhiking?" I said.

"What guy?" my dad replied.

The drop-kick kid was standing right there. How could my dad have not seen him? It didn't seem possible for the day to get any weirder.

A few blocks short of the freeway on-ramp, my dad turned into Parkway Fuel & Food, a twenty-four-hour gas station and convenience store franchise. He rolled up to a pump and cut the engine.

Lawrence took it as his cue to run the numbers. He peeled a blank sheet of paper from his pad and pulled a No. 2 pencil from the seven in his pocket protector. I could hear him scratching out the calculations before he announced his results.

"Fuel capacity: twenty-six gallons. Miles per gallon: twenty, highway. Miles to destination: one thousand five hundred and eighty-five. Fuel stops, including this one: four, maximum seven minutes per stop. Constant rate of speed necessary to arrive five minutes prior to the deadline, taking into account weather conditions, altitude, road topography, and engine efficiency: eighty miles per hour."

My dad pulled his wallet from his army jacket. "Here's twenty bucks. Go get yourselves some food. I'm gonna fill 'er up."

Dad handed the twenty to Lawrence, who tossed it over his shoulder into the back seat. "I have to stay here and guard my lunchbox. Please bring me one and three-quarter cups of hot water. I need my freeze-dried chili mac 'n' beef. I'm in training."

Lawrence operated under the belief that a freeze-dried brick of chili mac 'n' beef was the only meal astronauts ever ate. So consuming a steady diet of them would ensure his place on NASA's first mission to Mars.

When I stepped outside the truck, I noticed that the sun was setting, and the weather had turned chilly. I felt the cold air pressing against my face. I got halfway to the convenience store door when Lawrence rolled down his window and yelled additional instructions at me. "Bubblegum reinforcements! Make sure you get my brand: Bazooka Joe!"

"Anything else, sir?"

"Yeah. Get something for yourself too," he said, before rolling the window back up.

I was in such a hurry to get inside the convenience store that I bumped into an old man standing by the store's entrance. He was dirty and disheveled. He looked familiar, as if maybe I had seen him panhandling around town before.

"Pardon me, sir," I said, choosing not to burden him with a handshake.

The old man held out a plastic cup and looked me squarely in the eye. "Spare change for some food?"

"I'm sorry, but I've only got a twenty," I said as I darted to safety inside.

I poured Lawrence's fourteen ounces of hot water into a Styrofoam cup and put a lid on it. Then I grabbed a giant bag of Bazooka Joe, the kind of gum that comes with a comic wrapped around each individual piece. No doubt Lawrence honed his biting sense of humor by reading those four panels of cutting-edge comedy religiously.

I snagged two packs of beef jerky and a bag of barbecued potato chips for my dad. Then I went to the cold case and got myself a cheese sandwich and a bottle of my favorite drink, peach-flavored iced tea.

I was on my way to the cashier when I remembered that the old man had said he was hungry. I felt sorry for him. I went back to the cold case and got another cheese sandwich and peach-flavored iced tea.

"That'll be twenty-three fifty," said the clerk behind the counter. I checked my pockets for loose change as the line of impatient customers behind me grew longer.

I was flat broke.

"How much is it without one of the sandwiches?"

"Sandwiches are four bucks apiece. Give me nineteen fifty and we'll call it even."

The clerk took away the sandwich I couldn't afford, leaving me with the one I couldn't afford to go without. I handed him the twenty. He gave me two quarters in return and bagged up my food.

When I walked back outside, I was halfway hoping the old man had left. No such luck. He was still standing there holding his cup. I reached inside the bag and handed him one of the bottles of peach-flavored iced tea and both quarters.

"How did you know my favorite flavor is peach?"

Not only was the old man in need of a meal, but it seemed like he might be off his rocker too.

I took two steps toward the truck and stopped. My dad had finished pumping gas and was sitting in the driver's seat smoking another cigarette. Lawrence was watching me, his nose pressed up against the glass.

I reached back into the bag, handed the old man my cheese sandwich, and walked away.

"Thank you, Ezekiel."

43

We Stood and Stared
at Each Other

The old man's words stunned me. How did he know my name? He wasn't reading it off my name badge because Chip had made me turn in my polo shirt. Whenever anyone called me Ezekiel instead of Zeke, it meant I was in some sort of trouble. I felt my skin tingling. Reality seemed to warp a little, as if the old man and I were alone together in some sort of convenience store space-time continuum. I must have met the man before, I thought—maybe at the rec center, or at Chip's, or even at Wade's funeral.

By the time I was aware of my surroundings again, I was in the back seat of the truck, clutching the bag of food.

"The doctor is in!" Lawrence said. No doubt he was heaping praise on me for securing the key ingredient to his dinner.

I reached over and handed my dad his beef jerky and potato chips. Then I lobbed the jumbo bag of bubblegum over Lawrence's shoulder in the general direction of his lap.

"Hey!" Lawrence sounded annoyed.

I knew from past experience that when he got agitated, it would often activate his slapping hand. I went into damage containment mode. "Sorry, L.T. I'll make it up to you by not asking for much gum on the way to Kansas. I don't want to hog your supply."

I tried to pass Lawrence his cup of hot water, but he threw up his nonslapping hand as if to tell me to back off. When I peeked over his shoulder, I saw that his seven No. 2 pencils were no longer resting in formation inside his pocket protector. They were arranged on his lap in the now-familiar heptagonal configuration. I had a feeling that Lawrence might be using the geometric technique of neusis construction again to intercept 7th Dimension communiqués.

"He's been doing that since you walked into the store." It was clear my dad didn't know what to make of it, and he wasn't asking any questions.

"What's going on, buddy?" My instincts told me it was best to diffuse a potential crisis—or at least try to understand it.

"I thought he'd look a lot younger," Lawrence said.

"Who?"

"Him."

I had no idea what Lawrence was talking about. I handed him the cup. In a precision exercise, he snapped open his metal lunch crate and prepared his meal. Lawrence offered my dad a taste. Dad politely declined.

"We should probably get on the road," my dad said as he started the engine and dropped the transmission into gear. Dad got all the way to the driveway when Lawrence said it again.

"The doctor is in!"

I gazed at the old man through the window as I rummaged through all the murky places in my mind in search of a clue as to how I knew him, or how he knew me. No luck. It was like trying to remember a dream in the morning from the night before.

Dad turned onto the street and headed for the freeway. Just as the old man disappeared from view, it hit me.

"*Stop the truck!*"

My dad swerved to the curb and slammed on the brakes. I could see Lawrence bracing himself as the big Chevy skidded to a stop.

"What is it?" my dad demanded to know.

"I need to talk with him," I said as I kicked open the door and hotfooted it back to Parkway Fuel & Food.

When I got to the convenience store's front door, the old man was gone. I walked all the way around the building. There were lots of other people standing around, but he had vanished.

Lawrence and my dad had pulled back into the parking lot and were waiting for me in the truck. I was starting to sweat despite the crisp night air.

Then out of nowhere, I felt a tap on my shoulder. I whirled around and found myself standing face-to-face with the old man. His steely eyes met mine. I sensed he might be examining the parts of my soul where my dark secrets are tucked away for safekeeping.

He mumbled something that sounded like, "In order to fully understand the plight of these homeless souls, I must live among them."

"Excuse me, sir?"

"You never answered me," he said. "How did you know my favorite flavor is peach?"

I tried to speak but was unable to force any words out. The old man offered me a sip from the bottle of tea I had given him. It seemed to clear a passageway in my throat that had collapsed from mortal fear.

"You're him, aren't you?"

"Well, Ezekiel, I suppose I am."

My dad honked the horn a couple of times. I ignored it.

The last time I had seen the old man, he wasn't old at all. It was the previous year at Allen Fieldhouse, where he was in his thirties and had black hair parted in the center. His face then had been rugged and angular, but now his jowls had softened and rounded with age. He wore the same circular, old-school eyeglasses and had a bushy mustache. There was that same hint of a Canadian accent in his kind voice.

It was Dr. James Naismith.

But he wasn't the young man who had first appeared before me as the arena janitor. It was the Dr. Naismith I had seen in sports history books, the one who was photographed later in his life promoting the game of basketball around the United States and in Berlin, Germany, when basketball became an official Olympic event in 1936.

We stood and stared at each other. Dr. Naismith looked at me with what felt like compassion and understanding, while I could only gawk back at him in disbelief. I blurted out the first thing that popped into my head.

"Did I get you fired?"

"It is good to see you again, Ezekiel."

If ever there were a time to try out my new handshake, this was it. I dragged my hand across my pant leg to remove at least the top layer of sweat before reaching out to the elderly and possibly now homeless inventor of basketball. When I gripped his hand, I noticed that his skin was cracked and dirty. Nonetheless, I offered a sincere smile, looked him in the eye, and measured three gentle pumps over three seconds.

"I see you have been working on that," he said, his smile revealing a pressing need for dental work.

I was struggling to make sense of what in the world was going on. I should have already been on the freeway traveling to the middle of the country to confront the very man who was standing before me. I didn't know where to begin. I started to speak but was interrupted again.

"Is this man bothering you?"

44

Hurry Up. I'm Almost Out of Gum

It was heartening to see my father in the role of my father after he had all but abandoned me several years ago. His timing, however, was less than perfect.

"I've got this, Dad. Can you wait for me in the truck?"

I don't know whether it was out of nervousness or fear, but I decided to break the ice with the architect of basketball by trying out something Stretch might have said had he been standing next to me rather than slapping paint on an old warehouse somewhere.

"That overcoat makes you look ten years younger."

Dr. Naismith flashed a look of amusement. "It is good to see you too, Ezekiel. I appear older to you because my work here, this time around, is almost complete."

"This time around?"

"I understand you are looking for me." Dr. Naismith seemed intent on moving the conversation along.

He removed a vintage pocket watch from a torn trouser pocket. A miniature gold chain attached the watch to his soiled waistcoat. Dr. Naismith flipped open the spring-hinged, circular metal cover with his thumb and studied the hands beneath the crystal. He seemed to be on a schedule. That meant I must be too.

"What was it you wanted to talk with me about?"

I sensed that I might never have the opportunity again. I searched for the right words.

"My friend Lawrence keeps insisting that Wade's not dead."

"If I am not mistaken, your brother perished on the field of battle in Afghanistan, a brave casualty of an unfortunate war."

The tone of finality in Dr. Naismith's voice made me feel as though it might be pointless to pursue the conversation any further. I glanced over his shoulder toward the pickup. My dad was staring off into space, his hands folded on top of the steering wheel.

"I'm sorry to have taken up your—"

"Did your perceptive friend happen to mention a portal?"

A flicker of hope appeared.

"Yes! He said something about Wade's consciousness changing form when he died, something about solving the mystery by traveling through the 7th Dimension's portal.

Lawrence said you're the only one with the knowledge and wisdom to open that door."

"That sounds rather dramatic."

"You know Lawrence. Everything with him is eleven on a scale of ten."

Dr. Naismith took another peek at his pocket watch before having an extended look around. "It might not seem like much, but at least it has one of those gizmos for filling up your whitewalls with air."

"Wait a minute—you mean Parkway Fuel & Food is the top-secret portal?"

"Directly from 7th Dimension headquarters. We do not have much time. Perhaps you can start at the beginning and move it along swiftly."

In that moment, I knew we wouldn't have to drive all the way to Kansas, because the doctor had made a house call.

There wasn't a moment to lose. I explained everything that had happened to the best of my understanding, starting with the strange, dreamlike state I had fallen into while running a fast break at the regional basketball finals and again during summer tryouts at Jefferson. I told Dr. Naismith about all the people who were insisting they knew where the roads led. And how, according to Curtis, even a dolphin had gotten into the act.

"Dolphins serve as undersea messengers for the Entity," he said.

Those are words you don't often hear together in the same sentence.

Dr. Naismith told me that dolphins routinely watch over surfers as part of the harmonious relationship they enjoy while sharing ocean waves. He said that's why a dolphin was on hand to help Curtis out of a jam after he got buried beneath that colossal wave.

"The 7th Dimension tends to have quite a few plates spinning, so it looks for what we refer to as operational efficiencies," he said. "In your case, it seized the opportunity to deliver the all-roads message to you through Curtis, using the dolphin as a telepathic intermediary."

My head was swimming. If all roads led to Lawrence, why were we standing in Los Angeles? I asked Dr. Naismith. He explained that while the Entity does not knowingly put anyone in peril, its decisions often prompt individuals to take decisive and sometimes dangerous action.

He said the 7th Dimension felt it was prudent for our conversation to take place in the here and now rather than wait to see if we survived the marathon journey to Lawrence's namesake city with my dad driving the whole way like a power forward on a breakaway layup.

"It did not want a repeat performance of your dance with death last year across six states at speeds in excess of one hundred twenty-five miles per hour."

Dr. Naismith's mention of death opened the door for me to ask about Curtis's fate. "My friend who surfs, is he going to make it?"

"That is entirely up to Curtis. If he still has lessons to learn, he will pull through. If not, he will most assuredly travel the same path as Wade."

There wasn't much comfort in Dr. Naismith's assessment of Curtis's future. I had already lost my brother and my girlfriend—and pretty much my dad too, when I came to think about it, considering the long periods of time when he had mentally checked out of my life since leaving town. Though he was here with me now, I had to admit.

I thought about how much I relied on Stretch to keep things light, but he wasn't around anymore either, now that he had quit the team and dropped out of Jefferson to help out his dad.

I felt more alone than I ever had in my whole life.

"Our time is running short, Ezekiel." Dr. Naismith was beginning to look even older than he had when he first appeared in the parking lot out of thin air. "If there is anything else I can help you with, this would be a fine time to ask."

For a reason I cannot explain, Brock Decker was the next person who popped into my head. Even as I stood before a representative of the 7th Dimension, that cement-head was still tormenting me.

"I was wondering whether Brock and I might ever be friends again."

Dr. Naismith raised an eyebrow. His cheeks grew rosy as he smiled. "Everyone is on their own evolutionary path. Much of Brock's path leads steeply uphill, and there are many roadblocks to navigate." That was as good an explanation of the enigma that was Brock Decker as any I had ever heard. "And you have the power to help Brock, if you choose to."

Right. I would definitely have to think about that one.

I unloaded more questions on the doctor, starting with what had happened with Rebecca. I was messed up over the breakup. I asked Dr. Naismith for his insight.

"Perhaps it would be sensible to examine your relationship in basketball terms. There will be times on the court when you pass the ball away in order to get it back for a shot. In doing so, you are essentially setting something free that you love and trusting that it will return to you if you are open—if that is the right thing to happen."

From what I remembered about the conversation I had with Rebecca at Chip's, and from her letter, it sure seemed like she was never coming back.

"Another way to think about your relationship with Rebecca is to accept that you cannot force her to love you. Rather, you must allow Rebecca the freedom to choose."

Dr. Naismith's words rang true, but they only made the breakup hurt more. I tried to deaden the pain by changing the subject.

"What about my dad?"

"Kenton Archer is A-okay." That was Lawrence. He must have fallen from the sky, because I hadn't heard him step out of the truck.

Lawrence stood between Dr. Naismith and me, doing one of the things he did best: stating the obvious. "Your dad is in the truck staring through the windshield."

"It is nice to finally meet you, Sherman. You have caused the Entity, for lack of a better term, many sleepless nights."

"You look a lot older than I thought you would," Lawrence replied.

"As I have already explained to Ezekiel, I have quite nearly concluded my work during this cycle on Earth. Since my time here is measured as a physical manifestation of the human aging process, I now appear before you as I did on November 28, 1939."

I knew that date from the sports history book. It was when Dr. James Naismith had died. I knew we didn't have much time left with him.

"Hey, buddy, I'm almost done here. How about you go back and keep my dad company?"

"Hurry up. I'm almost out of gum."

45

It Was Now or Never

Lawrence turned to walk back to the truck, but he froze when he heard Dr. Naismith's voice.

"Sherman Tuckerman, thank you for your service to the Entity."

Lawrence reacted in a way I had never seen in him before. He beamed with pride.

"Well, Doc, it's always time to take action when there's danger," he said.

"Indeed, it is, young man."

Lawrence got back into the truck, slammed the door behind him, and flipped two more pieces of bubblegum into his mouth. All the while, my dad never moved a muscle. It seemed as if his mind were frozen in some other world. The real world, maybe.

I noticed Dr. Naismith shaking his head from side to side as he watched my dad study the inside of the truck's windshield.

"You asked me about your father," Dr. Naismith said, his tone turning somber. "I told you this when we first met, but it bears repeating now: violence as a means of resolving conflict does not work."

I remembered those words, not because Dr. Naismith had offered them inside Allen Fieldhouse the previous year but because they were the basis for rule number five of his Original 13 Rules of Basketball.

Rule number five calls for the disqualification of any player who shows evident intent to injure another person. Dr. Naismith's reference at the time was to the violent act I had committed at the high school finals, which had only led to pain and heartache.

"Your father has witnessed man's inhumanity to man firsthand. He has seen things, done things on the battlefield that he is unable to forget."

Dr. Naismith said that the Entity's introduction of basketball on Earth in 1891 was one of the strategic measures it employed to counteract tiny errors embedded in the programming of humankind's DNA that can cause people to commit acts of evil.

"Your father is not the same person he was before he left home to fight for his country," Dr. Naismith said. "Part of him perished on the front lines, I am sad to say."

I remembered my mom telling me when Dad returned home from the Iraq War how much he had changed. I didn't understand it at the time, but Dr. Naismith's words of wisdom helped me to see my dad as the whole person he really was now.

The momentary silence was broken by the sound of Lawrence's power window rolling down. He stuck his skinny arm outside and launched a paper airplane right at us. The tiny aircraft caught a light breeze and climbed before descending and landing at our feet. When I reached down to pick it up, I saw that it was an airworthy folded-up five-dollar bill.

"Your friend Mr. Tuckerman has a future in aviation," Dr. Naismith said with certainty.

"Gum!" Lawrence made it clear that his supply was running low. "And get something for yourself too."

I unfolded the money and stuffed it into my pocket. When I looked back at Dr. Naismith, it seemed as though he had aged even more and was significantly weaker than he had been only moments before. The lines across his forehead had grown deeper. He was hunched over and shivering. His breathing was shallow.

"Are you okay, sir?"

"I am afraid my time here is running short, Ezekiel. Is there anything else before I go?"

So much had happened since we pulled into the gas station that I had almost forgotten why we were driving to 7th Dimension headquarters to begin with. I knew I was almost out of time.

"What can you tell me about my brother? Lawrence said Wade was still alive because of the math, but I don't know what that means, and Lawrence isn't good at explaining complicated stuff."

Dr. Naismith struggled to breathe and staggered backward. I lunged forward to catch him, but too late. He was headed for the hard pavement when a metal post holding up a sign that read No Loitering caught his fall. He steadied himself. I handed him his bottle of peach-flavored iced tea. He took a few sips and gave it back to me.

"I am not sure you are ready for the truth about your brother," he said, his voice growing weaker.

My instincts told me it was now or never.

"With all due respect, sir, I was ready for the truth when I asked you the first time."

46

This Is Bigger Than Basketball

The closest I had ever come to witnessing death was the alternate-reality encounter I had with Wade in a desert fighting hole after running a perfectly executed fast break during basketball tryouts.

I still wasn't sure if what had happened then was real, but watching the lifeforce drain from Dr. Naismith right before my eyes was scaring the living crap out of me.

"Help me down," Dr. Naismith said.

I gripped his hand and guided him gently down to the concrete walkway, his back leaning against the convenience store's graffiti-covered brick wall. Dr. Naismith's skin was pale. His breathing grew shallower.

"I'm going to call an ambulance!"

"That will not be necessary, Ezekiel. Our time together is coming to an end. Please listen carefully, as there will not be another opportunity. Your friend Lawrence is a savant, a young man of profound learning. He has used his unique autistic powers to tap into the 7th Dimension's connection to universal knowledge."

All that time, I had thought Lawrence was just another nerdy math genius who ate freeze-dried brick food and had a profound desire to travel to a distant planet.

"Lawrence leveraged his deep knowledge of biomathematics to prove that your brother did not die. Rather, Wade has made a significant change of address."

Dr. Naismith's words made no sense. I told him to save his strength, but he kept talking. He reinforced Lawrence's earlier words about human consciousness being a form of energy that existed as a fundamental element of the universe and outside the constraints of time and space.

"Lawrence once told you that energy could neither be created nor destroyed—it can only change form," Dr. Naismith said. "The truth is, your friend knows much that he has not yet learned. The knowledge he has shared with you is only the beginning. The fruit is already within the seed."

I felt as if I were being buried alive under a mountain of incomprehensible coded messages from the future.

Dr. Naismith's eyelids drooped. He fell forward, but I caught him before he could bonk his head against the sidewalk. When I shook his shoulders, he came to.

"That's enough, sir. We need to get you to a hospital."

Dr. Naismith held up a hand in protest. "No time."

His other hand trembled as it gripped his pocket watch. He studied it before letting go, the gold chain catching its fall.

"When Lawrence stumbled onto the Entity's communications system, the Entity knew it could not undo his actions nor take away his knowledge, so it devised a way for Lawrence to understand the Entity's power and mission by giving it a mathematically accessible name—hence, the '7th Dimension.'"

I felt the hairs lifting up on the back of my neck.

"You must try your best to understand what I am about to tell you."

My ears were taking in the words, but my brain didn't know what to do with them. I was in the presence of a dying man, and I was hanging onto the conversation by my fingernails.

"Lawrence's conclusions were crude but accurate," Dr. Naismith said. "Ezekiel, this is bigger than basketball."

47

This Was *Always* About Basketball

Out of the corner of my eye, I noticed Lawrence approaching. He was race-walking, so I figured he would have a full head of steam by the time he arrived. I tried to get out in front. "I know, more gum. I'm on that."

"Kenton Archer says we need to hit the road this exact instant if we're going to make it to Kansas in time. Hey, does the old guy have any gum?"

Dr. Naismith shook his head. I knew there was no time for an extended conversation with Lawrence, so I tried to walk him back to the truck. Lawrence took a couple of steps and stopped.

"Check his pockets," Lawrence said. "He might be holding out on us."

"I really don't think that's a good idea."

Lawrence flashed a micro-smile. It was identical to the one he had unveiled as he revealed the biomathematical formula on all those sheets of paper in his bedroom.

"Did you get Dr. Naismith fired? Is that why he's homeless?"

"You are not the first person to ask that question." Dr. Naismith had overheard our conversation.

"Get back in the truck, *now*," I said.

"It's called humor," Lawrence said. "Look it up in the dictionary."

Lawrence had picked a bad time to emerge from his shell. I heard the truck door slam as I rejoined Dr. Naismith on the sidewalk.

Dr. Naismith continued his lecture: "At the risk of bogging you down with too many facts, Earth's scientists theorize that there are ten billion galaxies in what is known as the observable universe. By observable, I am referring only to what scientists can perceive as a result of the Big Bang, which occurred 13.8 billion years ago."

"Yes, sir."

Dr. Naismith was hallucinating. I wanted to be there for him the way I had been there for Wade when he was bleeding to death in the fighting hole.

"With an average of one hundred billion stars—similar to Earth's sun, mind you— per galaxy, the math works out to the existence of roughly one sextillion stars. A sextillion is a one followed by seven sets of three zeroes. *Seven* sets."

Geez, more sevens. There was no escaping them. If Dr. Naismith and I had been sitting on the sidewalk playing poker during our conversation about the origins and nature of the universe, sevens would have been wild.

"Here is where it gets complicated," Dr. Naismith said.

The truth was, my life had started to get complicated the moment I took a swing at Brock Decker and walloped a referee instead.

Dr. Naismith's breathing grew labored, his voice barely rising above a whisper. "Let us look at this in basketball terms. The universe is home court. The 7th Dimension is the head coach. I am an assistant coach. You and Curtis and Stretch are the players, as are all lifeforms circling the stars in all of the galaxies in the universe."

"Yes, sir." I knew there had to be a reasonable explanation for all the weirdness that had surrounded me ever since I set off a near riot at the high school finals.

"You see, Ezekiel, this was *always* about basketball."

My heart wanted to take it on faith that what he was saying was true, but my head was screaming that it was impossible.

"Is that guy all right?" It was the store clerk, his eyebrows squishing together as he gawked at the homeless version of the creator of basketball. "Maybe I should call the police."

"That will not be necessary, kind sir. I am fine."

I knew that Dr. Naismith was anything but.

"Whatever," the clerk said as he went back inside the store.

My intuition was telling me there wasn't much time left. Putting Dr. Naismith's universal blueprint aside, I still didn't know what Lawrence meant by telling me that he knew Wade wasn't dead because of the math.

"Sir, what about my brother?"

Dr. Naismith gasped for air. He coughed and choked and tried in vain to steady himself. His voice was now barely audible. He spoke to me in a whisper. "Everything in the universe is interconnected," he croaked. "Not just some things. Everything. *Every thing.* All objects in the universe retain evidence of every event that ever occurred. The Entity's laws allow the human mind to retrieve that evidence."

I was still clinging onto my hope that Dr. Naismith's crazy theories would make any kind of sense, and more importantly, have anything to do with Wade.

"Your brother died in *your* reality, not in his."

48

There Is So Much More to Tell You, But Our Time Has Run Short

I heard the faint wail of a siren off in the distance. The convenience store clerk must have phoned for help.

My father tapped the horn to get my attention and lowered the passenger side window. Lawrence, sitting beside him, ducked as my dad shouted, "C'mon, Zeke, we gotta go!"

I waved him off again.

Dr. Naismith tried and failed to straighten his body, which was twisted and slouched against the store wall. "Eternity does not have a deadline," he said.

Still more gibberish. There was no way Dr. Naismith would live long enough to explain what had happened to Wade. I just knew it.

Dr. Naismith seemed to gather together whatever remaining strength he had. "All consciousness in the universe was created eons ago in the Big Bang," he said. "Wade's physical death was not the end of his consciousness, because all consciousness is infinite, without beginning or end."

Dr. Naismith might as well have been speaking a foreign language. I barely understood anything he was saying. The vehicle with the blaring siren was getting closer.

"I'm sorry, sir, but I don't know what that *means*."

"Wade's brain was an organ for selecting and transmitting his consciousness rather than for generating it. His consciousness exists beyond space and time. It survived his physical death."

Dr. Naismith's words scared the crap out of me, not because they were those of a dying man but because they went against every core belief about life and death I had ever held.

I had seen death firsthand when I stood over a six-foot hole in the ground at Southland Meadows Memorial Park as cemetery workers lowered Wade's casket into the earth for eternity. I knew it was possible that Dr. Naismith's bizarre ramblings were due to a lack of oxygen, but I didn't care. I refused to believe him. I needed to tell him so.

"I don't think any of that is true, sir."

Dr. Naismith lifted his cheeks in a good-hearted smile. When he did, drool ran down his chin. "People often avoid things they do not understand," he said. "You are not required to know how something works in order to accept that it exists. If that were the case, some of mankind's greatest inventions and works of art would never have been created."

When I persisted in questioning his theories, he told me that my doubt was based on the human mind's limited belief that something must cause something else to happen.

"It's just not so, sir. I know my consciousness is locked inside my brain, because I see and hear and taste and smell everything through my head, and my brain is inside my head."

"Coincidence, pure and simple, Ezekiel. Trying to comprehend consciousness by investigating what is inside your skull is like trying to understand the game of basketball by taking apart the ball and analyzing its rubber parts."

The next sound I heard was the screeching of tires as an LA County Fire Department ambulance bounced and skidded into the parking lot.

"There is so much more to tell you, but our time has run short. I will leave you with this: Free will allows for dying human beings to have one final opportunity to connect with someone before they cross over to the other side. That is why you encountered your brother in the fighting hole. It was closure—for Wade."

Curtis had told me about free will after he learned about it in his philosophy class at Jefferson. I understood it to be the power of a person to make a choice that was not predestined by fate or divine will.

My father jumped out of the pickup and raced toward us. Lawrence rolled his window back up, no doubt to simulate bedroom conditions by barricading himself inside.

I could hear the fire department dispatcher dishing out coded commands through the loudspeaker on top of the red emergency vehicle.

Dr. Naismith drew in a deep, raspy breath and slumped to the sidewalk.

"Over here!" I shouted to the paramedics.

The gentle old man, who I had known first as the Allen Fieldhouse janitor and had later come to respect as the humble inventor of the greatest game on Earth, exhaled one last time and fell silent as the pink life faded from his face.

He was dead.

49

You're Not Supposed to Be Here

One of the paramedics bent down and slid the diaphragm of her stethoscope inside Dr. Naismith's waistcoat. She listened for signs of life, but it was clear she found none. She shook her head and motioned for the other paramedic to bring the gurney.

The world seemed to slow down around me. My eyelids felt gummy. Dad wrapped his arm around my shoulder as the paramedics lifted Dr. Naismith onto the stretcher, covered his body with a white sheet, and loaded him into the back of the ambulance.

"Who was he?" my dad asked.

"Just an old friend. I met him through basketball." I knew I couldn't tell my dad about my connection to Dr. Naismith.

The ambulance drove across the parking lot in less of a hurry than when it arrived. The lights were still flashing, but the siren was silent. I figured there was no rush to take Dr. Naismith to the county morgue.

Lawrence exited the truck and walked over to join us. "Here," he said, handing me a wedge of bubblegum. "This will help."

"I can't. You're running low."

"It's okay. I still have a few left."

The three of us kept vigil as the ambulance merged into heavy afternoon traffic. I was distracted by something that splashed off the top of my head. I looked up and saw that it had started to rain. By the time the ambulance had faded from sight, the sky opened up and we were standing in a downpour. If I didn't know better, I would have thought the gods were crying.

"C'mon, we've got a lot of highway ahead of us," my dad said.

Not anymore. I explained to my father in vague terms that we no longer needed to drive to Kansas because there had been a sudden change in plans. Dad didn't ask any questions. Either he didn't want to know the reason, or he was too road weary to ask.

Alone in the back seat, I was hypnotized by the squeak-thump of the windshield wipers as we drove Lawrence home. After we dropped him off, I jumped into the front seat and asked my dad to take me back to the hospital so I could square things with my mom.

Dad made a U-turn as I tried to reconcile what I had

witnessed at the gas station. There was so much information to process, I didn't know where to begin.

I grasped that there are billions of galaxies in something called the observable universe, but was I supposed to take it on faith that my brother's consciousness existed somewhere out there beyond the limits of space and time? And what about my one and only chance to connect with Wade before he crossed over to the other side? The other side of *what*? And if that were somehow real, how could I live with myself after failing to stop my brother from bleeding to death? Wade would have found a way to save *my* life if the circumstances had been reversed.

"We're here."

I had lost track of time. Dad stepped out of the truck and stood in front of the hospital's main entrance. I flung my backpack over my shoulder and pulled my wet bike from the truck bed.

"Sorry you drove all the way here for nothing. Guess I'll see you later."

"I love you, son."

My stomach muscles clenched as I watched my dad's truck turn the corner and disappear from view. It shot me back in time to when he left our family for good and moved to Denver.

I took inventory of my life, thinking it might distract me from the gnawing feeling in my gut: no father, no brother, no basketball team, no girlfriend, no job, no chance at a basketball guardianship, one best friend in a coma, and another who might as well be because he could no longer pursue his dream.

I locked up my bike and tracked rainwater into the hospital lobby. I needed to tell my mom that the trip to the University of Kansas was canceled. I was hoping she would ask me as many questions as my dad had.

The guard must have sensed I was having a miserable day, because he handed me my badge and waved me through without the usual interrogation, just as he had when I last visited. I went to the third-floor nurse's station to look for my mom, but no one was there, so I kept going until I got to the entrance to the ICU.

I checked to make sure the coast was clear and ducked inside. I spotted Curtis in the same place as before. He seemed even more frail than when I had seen him about an hour earlier.

After what had happened at the gas station, I knew all too well what it was like to be standing next to a person who didn't have much time left. I was getting that same eerie feeling in my bones as I stood over my friend and the network of tubes that crisscrossed his body.

Maybe Curtis would have been better off if the dolphin had let him drown. At least he would've been at peace instead of lying there like a human pincushion with little active brain function.

I slid a chair over to the side of Curtis's bed and sat down for a one-sided conversation.

"Who's going to try to teach me how to surf, even though I have zero interest in learning? And who's always going to have my back, no matter what? Jed Swagerty? Mrs. Fenner?"

No answer. None expected.

"How are we supposed to go three-on-three at the rec center with just two guys? We both know that Stretch couldn't hit a jumper from more than five feet away if his life depended on it."

Still nothing.

"Guess I'll have to give your spot to Brock Decker, even though once I pass the ball to him, I'll never see it again, because that ball hog never, ever passes."

That last remark must have cut through the fog. I thought I heard Curtis moan through his oxygen mask, and it looked as though he might have wiggled one pinkie.

Just then, my mother busted through the ICU door.

"You're not supposed to be here," she said.

"I can explain."

"I thought you were on your way to Kansas."

"I thought I saw Curtis move."

My mom seemed surprised. She checked Curtis's chart and adjusted his oxygen mask. Mom raised an eyebrow when she took his pulse and checked his heartbeat, as if she had noticed a change in his condition. When she put her hand on Curtis's forehead, he blinked and popped his eyes open.

Mom jumped back in surprise.

My heart went up three floors to my throat.

Curtis rocked his head from side to side as if he were trying to shake off the mask—and the cobwebs. My mom pried the device from over his mouth and nose.

Curtis looked me in the eye and spoke in a scratchy whisper. "No way, bro. That cement-head's not taking *my* spot."

50

I Needed to Get My Job Back

Within two minutes, the ICU was filled with doctors and nurses shaking their heads in disbelief. Curtis had gone from death's doorstep to hospital-wing celebrity status in the course of my brief visit. If a hospital orderly had lugged a surfboard into the ICU, my friend would have been asked to autograph it.

Curtis flashed me the shaka sign, a time-honored hand gesture meant to convey a surfer's friendly intent. I had also seen Curtis use the gesture to invite a friend to hang loose. I knew I wouldn't be hanging loose anytime soon, because I had a considerable amount of fence-mending to do.

I gave my mom a hug and told her I had to go but would be home in time for dinner. Curtis caught my eye and motioned me over.

"Dude, do you think Brock Decker and the dolphin are the same person? I've never seen them at a party together."

It was clear Curtis was still getting his bearings, and there would be much rehab in his future. I fist-bumped him and rode the elevator back down to the lobby. I needed to get my job back at Chip's if I had any hope of ever driving my brother's antique Chevy again.

When I stepped outside the hospital, I was met by heavier rainfall than when my father had dropped me off. But it wasn't going to stop me. I had to get to Chip's. The only way there was to ride my bike across town in a summer monsoon.

I arrived at the front door of Chip's Sporting Goods just before closing time, soaked to the gills and shivering. I wheeled my bike into the foyer and leaned it up against the wall. Nathan was at the register ringing up a customer when he noticed me. He yelled something in my general direction after he completed the transaction, but I couldn't hear what he said over the sound of my teeth chattering. He left the register and marched over to where I was standing.

"Who's going to mop that up?" Nathan demanded, pointing to the pool of rainwater I had deposited onto the Chip's logo in the lobby. Nathan caught me staring at his name badge, which no longer read Assistant Supervisor.

"Is Chip around?" I asked.

"I'm the *senior* assistant supervisor. What is this in regard to?"

"Nathan, it's me."

Nathan had moved up the ranks fast. He must have benefited from my unexpected departure a couple of hours earlier.

"Mr. Spears is indisposed. Is there something I can help you with?"

Nathan was really working me over. "I came to talk to Chip about getting my job back."

"I'm not sure that's possible, Mr. Archer. Your recent departure didn't sit well with senior management and created quite a burden on the store's rank and file."

Nathan wasn't budging. He was leaving me no choice but to consider taking my lack of marketable job skills elsewhere.

"Is everything all right here, Nathan?"

It was Chip. He must have heard the commotion from his office in the back of the store.

"It's nothing, just Zeke groveling for his old job back. Since the ink on his termination papers isn't even dry yet, I told him that his request for reinstatement would likely be denied."

Chip walked over and extended his hand. "Chip Spears. I understand you're seeking employment."

"Yes, sir." Every inch of my clothing was soggy, so I had nowhere to wipe my hand. That left me no choice but to take hold of Chip's hand for three squishy pumps. He wiped his hand on his shirt sleeve and motioned for me to follow him to his office.

When we arrived, he pulled my personnel file from a cabinet and asked me to take a seat. Chip lectured me on the competitive nature of the sporting goods industry and how he had a responsibility to enforce workplace rules that would ensure the store's survival, for the good of customers and employees alike.

"We're fending off Global Mega-Sports at every turn," he said. "I pay our people a fair wage, and I expect everyone to work hard and commit to excellence."

"Yes, sir."

Chip told me that my decision to leave the company after only two weeks on the job had put him behind the eight ball. He said he had needed to promote Nathan to senior assistant supervisor just to keep employee morale from plummeting.

"Nathan was crushed when I had to terminate your employment for cause. He really enjoyed working with you."

That came as news to me. Nathan seemed agitated whenever I was around him. Our only common ground aside from arguing with each other was our friendship with Lawrence.

"Are we talking about the same Nathan?"

Chip pulled a wrinkled, nearly new polo shirt from his desk drawer.

"Here, you might recognize this." The polo still had my name badge pinned to it. "Since you've only been gone for a couple of hours, I'm going to let you keep your level of seniority. Report to work tomorrow at 9:00 a.m. *Sharp.*"

I walked past the chess and checkers section on my way out the door. Nathan was there restocking the shelves. He seemed less irritated than usual. I told him that Chip had generously reinstated me.

"See you tomorrow, rookie."

51

A Wave of Nausea Shoved Aside the Gnawing in My Gut

It was well into the evening when I took off for Jefferson Community College in the driving rain. Every time I thought it wasn't possible to take on more water, another car would cruise by and dump an avalanche of sludgy runoff all over me.

All along Chamberlain Drive, I saw homeless encampments under bridges and in the corners of parking lots. No doubt the deluge was adding to the misery of life on the streets. It reminded me of the work Dr. Naismith said he had been doing when I encountered him at the gas station.

I had memorized the basketball team's summer schedule, so I knew that practice had ended hours earlier. There was no guarantee Coach Kincaid would still be on campus.

I turned into Jefferson's main entrance and pedaled through six inches of standing water all the way to the gymnasium. The parking lot was a waterlogged ghost town. I yanked on the door handle to the gym. Given everything else that was going on in my life, I was unsurprised to discover that I was locked out. I banged on the door in quest of a miracle. None came.

My last resort was Coach Kincaid's office. I entered the PE building and sloshed down the hallway. As I approached the coach's office, I could hear the clickety-clack of what sounded like an old-school typewriter.

The door was open. I knocked and took a step inside. Coach stopped typing and looked up from his desk.

"My goodness, Zeke, you're soaking wet. What'd you do, ride here on your bike?"

"Yes, sir."

Coach reached into a canvas bag that held the team's gym towels. Those towels were standard issue for community college athletic programs. They were as soft as sandpaper and equally as absorbent.

"Take two, they're small."

"Thanks, Coach."

Coach Kincaid went back to his desk as I moved the water around on my clothing.

"Can you sit tight for a few minutes? I just need to finish what I'm working on."

"Sure thing, Coach."

Coach resumed his two-fingered clickety-clacking while I did all I could to avoid ruining his guest chair. When he finished typing, he zip-thunked the typewriter's manual carriage return a few times until a sheet of paper ejected from the top. Coach made no attempt to conceal his concern. "Is everything all right? I thought you were leaving town."

"That was the plan, but things changed pretty fast."

I remembered Coach's disappointment when I told him I couldn't attend practice because I had to hit the road. I thought he would be happy that I had stayed in Los Angeles, but I was wrong. He looked even more uneasy than he had a couple of hours earlier. I was about to ask about my roster spot, but he beat me to it.

"I told you when you left that I'd be making final roster decisions after practice. I always type my rosters on that old relic because it's difficult to use, so it feels like I'm making more of a *commitment* to my players."

"Yes, sir."

Coach Kincaid's heavy emphasis on the word *commitment* wasn't lost on me. He got up from his chair and handed me that piece of paper. I wasn't ready for life without basketball.

"I'm on my way to post that on the bulletin board in the locker room. I'm sorry, Zeke, but the team had to move on without you."

It felt like I must be visibly sweating, but I figured Coach hadn't noticed because I was still soaked from the stormy ride over. A wave of nausea shoved aside the gnawing in my gut.

I scanned the top of the list, hoping Coach had alphabetized it by last name and was playing a practical joke on me. *Archer* wasn't there. Then I jumped to the bottom on the off-chance he had ordered the roster by first name and had somehow hunted-and-pecked *Zeke* by mistake without an eraser handy, so he could have no choice but to let me play. No such luck.

Brock Decker's and Jed Swagerty's names were there, of course. Curtis's and Stretch's weren't, but I wasn't expecting them to be. I returned the list to Coach.

"I need players who are willing to commit to this team. I'm sorry things didn't work out. I hope you'll come out to a few games during the season. It's always nice to see a friendly face in the crowd."

I reached out my hand to Coach Kincaid. I knew it was still wet, but I set that aside in favor of offering him my best version of the Chip Spears handshake.

We walked out of his office in opposite directions.

Before I left the building, I heard his voice echoing down the hallway. "We've got an opening for a team manager, if you're interested."

Team manager. *Wow.* I didn't know that rock bottom had a basement.

52

Care to Comment on *That*?

"What do you think?" Coach Kincaid seemed to want an answer right away.

I had never paid much attention to the role of the team manager during my freshman season at Jefferson, nor while I played at Southland Central High. From what I remembered, the team manager was a kid with more enthusiasm than athletic skills who passed out water and towels during practices and games.

"What would I need to do?"

"It's an important job—hand out water and towels, mostly."

I wasn't sure whether my sense of pride would allow me to take the job, but I had already let down Coach one time too many to say no.

"I guess I can do it."

"So, that's a yes?"

"Yes, sir."

Coach Kincaid said he would need me to attend basketball practice for the rest of the summer. Then I would have to enroll in Jefferson's sports management class for the upcoming semester. That meant I would have the chance to be close to the game I loved, but not close enough to have a basketball in my hands.

I said goodbye to Coach Kincaid and exited the PE building. I was surprised to see that the rain had stopped. It was an unexpected bright spot in an otherwise crappy day.

On the bike ride home across flooded streets, all I could think about was how basketball no longer filled the empty hole inside me. The farther away I pedaled from the Jefferson gym, the more it felt like my life would be on a different course.

"Cheese and crackers, Zeke!" Mrs. Fenner had accosted me again. "Why are you riding that confounded thing in weather like this when you could be driving one of those perfectly good clunkers in the carport?"

"I'm working on it, Mrs. Fenner."

By the time I had dragged my bike up the stairs and into my apartment, I had made a decision, the kind that changes your life in an instant.

I was quitting basketball.

Without Curtis and Stretch to share the court, and without my brother around to watch over me, there was nothing left to play for. I had to serve as Jackrabbits team manager because I had committed to the job. But the fact was, I was burnt out on the game.

Stick a fork in me. I was done.

Life got back to normal—a new normal.

I spent the rest of the summer at Chip's being bossed around by Nathan so I could earn enough money to afford car insurance.

I enrolled in six courses for the fall semester at Jefferson. It was a heavy load, but all I wanted to do was bury myself in my studies so there wouldn't be any time left over to feel sorry for myself.

Curtis had gone into a rehab program and was regaining his strength. He wasn't back on a surfboard quite yet, but he was spending a lot of time at Zuma soaking up the energy coming off the waves.

Stretch worked for his dad all summer, so I rarely saw him, although Curtis told me Stretch had managed to get to the Jefferson gym on his lunch hour now and then to shoot around.

My mom continued to work tons of overtime at the hospital, so our paths didn't cross much at home. I hadn't heard a word from my dad since he returned to Denver. As far as things with Rebecca were concerned, it was radio silence.

"I understand you didn't make the cut this season. Care to comment?"

It was the first day of the new semester. I had just parked Wade's truck in the parking lot and was about to walk into my journalism class when the *Jefferson Journal*'s intrepid sports reporter Darla Davenport planted herself in front of me to block the doorway, pad and pencil in hand.

"No comment, Darla."

"That sounded like a *resounding* 'No comment' to me."

As usual, Darla had put herself in position to get the scoop. Her timing was unwelcome.

"Other guys were more committed to the team than I was, so I signed on as team manager."

"Team manager?"

"Yeah, it's a lot like covering the team for the school paper, but without the pencil, and I don't have to be as annoying."

Darla jotted it all down while I looked at my watch to see how much longer I would have to endure the impromptu interview before the bell rang.

"What about Stretch?" Darla said.

"What about him?"

"I understand he re-enrolled and made the team. Care to comment on *that*?"

Sure, I had a comment: What on Earth was Darla talking about?

53

That's Your Team in the Bag

There was no way Stretch had time to play basketball at Jefferson, let alone attend classes there. I also knew that Stretch would have told me if he were trying out for the team.

I spent the school day in a fog wandering from class to class until I walked into the gym for the first official practice of the season. One by one, all thirteen players who had made the team came out of the locker room to warm up. Stretch was the last to step onto the court. He pretended not to notice me, but I was quicker than he was and beat him to the ignore.

"Yo, towel boy! Get me a lemonade with one of those tiny umbrellas in it, easy on the ice."

"Shut up, Brock."

I kept myself busy with water-and-towel distribution duties while Coach Kincaid ran the players through drills that focused on fundamentals and team building.

Stretch moved with more agility and finesse than I could remember, and his hook shot was fluid and accurate. He also seemed taller than the last time I had hung out with him.

At the end of practice, Coach Kincaid blew his whistle and waved the team to center court as I slouched on the sideline hanging my head.

"C'mon, Zeke, you're a part of this team too," Coach said.

"Never underestimate the importance of an attentive water boy when you're parched," Brock whispered under his breath as I approached.

Back in the day, I would have stood nose to nose with Brock after a crack like that, but I was too demoralized to respond.

"Nice job out there today, gentlemen," Coach Kincaid said. "Same time tomorrow. Get some rest."

As I turned to walk away in the opposite direction from where the team was heading—the locker room—I saw Brock out of the corner of my eye attempting to snap me on the butt with a towel. Stretch reached down, caught the coarse fabric in midflight, and yanked it right out of Brock's hand.

"Grow up, cement-head," Stretch said. "Have some respect for team management."

Brock and Jed smirked and peeled off for the lockers while I headed for the exit.

"Zeke!" Stretch called out my name, but I had no interest in talking with him. "Hey, man, it's me." Stretch's elongated face seemed even longer than usual.

"I almost didn't recognize you. Did you grow?"

"Yeah, I'm seven-three now."

I explained to Stretch how surprised I was to see him on the court. The last time we had talked, he had just quit the team and dropped out of school. He told me he had made arrangements with his father to take an extended lunch hour every day to work out at Jefferson. Stretch said that after a while, Coach Kincaid noticed his dedication, and they discussed the possibility of his rejoining the team.

"Coach likes having a big man in the post," he said.

Stretch told me that Coach Kincaid had helped him get into a couple of summer school evening classes to re-establish his eligibility.

"What about this semester?"

"I'm enrolled in four criminal justice courses at night. Between school and practice and helping my dad paint, it doesn't leave time for much else."

After a few weeks, I had settled into a mind-numbing pattern of daydreaming through my classes, taking verbal abuse from Brock in practice, and listening to Nathan chew me out at work. I was on autopilot, going through the motions while the world slapped me on the side of the head as it passed me by.

Then one afternoon at the sporting goods store, everything changed.

"Dude, which way to the surf section?"

It was Curtis. I hadn't seen him in a few weeks. Rehab was agreeing with him. He looked clear-eyed and healthy. I knew he had enrolled in oceanography and philosophy classes at Jefferson. After Curtis's recent underwater experiences with cetacean mysticism, that sounded like an ideal combination of classes for him.

"What are you doing here?"

"Do those polo shirts come in aloha style?"

Curtis had stopped by Chip's to fill me in on his recovery. He said he was not yet surfing, but every morning before school he was driving to Zuma to paddle around on his surfboard in shallow water. "Baby steps, bud."

"I'd better get back to work before Nathan sees me slacking off."

"I need a favor."

Curtis knew I would do anything for him. He only had to name it.

"How about doing *me* a favor by letting Zeke do his job?"

Foiled again! By Nathan's innate knack for knowing when I was goofing off.

"We've got a business to run here."

"Back off and scratch it, landlubber," Curtis snapped. "Ezekiel was just showing me to the board wax."

Nathan stormed off as Curtis and I zigzagged through the store to the surfing gear.

"Whoa, Dude Duderson is pretty worked up," Curtis said.

"Nathan's cool. He's got a lot on his mind. What do you need?"

Curtis said he had been shooting baskets as part of his therapy while recovering from the surfing accident. He asked if I could stop by the rec center after work to rebound for him. "My shot's coming back. Just need you to park under the basket and shag the leather for me as it glides through."

We set a time to meet at the rec center, and Curtis took off. Nathan didn't say another word to me until we ran into each other in the break room.

"What's up, rookie?"

I pulled an American cheese sandwich on egg bread from my locker as Nathan chomped down on baked chess pieces from a plastic bag. When he finished, he stuffed the empty bag into his backpack. Then he pulled out a full one and tossed it across the table.

"I asked Grammy to bake those for you."

I opened the bag and found bread figurines inside. They weren't chess pieces. They were basketball players, five of them.

"What are these for?"

I remembered Nathan saying his grandmother baked her chess pieces using an ancestral baking formula that helped him to shake off his anger before it could take root.

"Grammy used ingredients that'll absorb whatever's crawling around inside you that makes you so unhappy. That's your team in the bag. The one with the extra-crispy head is Brock."

54

Welcome Back, Bro

I thanked Nathan for his kindness, asked him to thank his grandmother for me, and washed down my cheese sandwich with all five basketball player bread figurines. Yes, that's right, I ate the whole starting lineup. Biting Brock's toasty head off was curiously satisfying. This is going to sound weird, but for the first time in a long while, I began to feel normal again.

I finished my shift and drove to the rec center to meet up with Curtis. On my way to the outdoor basketball court, I stopped by the office to check in with Mr. Shields.

"I heard Stretch is back on the team." Mr. Shields had been the head coach at Jefferson for twenty-five years before he retired and Coach Kincaid took over the program. Even though Mr. Shields had been away from the college for a few years, it was clear he still had connections there.

"Yeah, I've seen him in practice," I said. "His game's really improving."

"I'd imagine you're seeing a lot of things in practice as team manager," Mr. Shields said. "Are you playing much ball yourself?"

I explained to Mr. Shields that I had decided to step away from the game for a while to focus on schoolwork and my part-time job at Chip's.

Mr. Shields looked at me with an analytical eye. "That could explain why you seem a little out of shape."

"I might have put on a couple of pounds."

Mr. Shields had just given me a wakeup call for which I was not prepared. Being out of shape was one of the unintended consequences of my decision to quit basketball. It was clear I hadn't thought it all the way through.

"I figure you're here to work with Curtis. He sure has come a long way since the accident. I know he can really use your help."

I gave Mr. Shields my well-honed Chip Spears handshake and made my way to the court. Curtis was there playing three-on-three with some of the rec center regulars. He was not yet the Curtis of old, but his passes were sharp, and he was moving with relative ease. One of the other kids noticed me walk in.

"Zeke, you got next?"

"No. I'm here to work out with Curtis when you guys are done."

My presence seemed to give Curtis a lift. On his team's next possession, he called for the ball and buried a rainmaker from the top of the key. Then he followed it up with two more long-range jumpers from downtown.

"Ballgame!" Curtis said.

The other guys all shook hands and went back inside the rec center. Curtis toweled the sweat from his face and plopped down on a bench to catch his breath.

"You looked good out there."

"Shot's falling. Rest of my game's got a long way to go."

"You said you needed me to rebound for you?"

"I'm kinda spent, dude. Just need to talk."

Curtis told me he had been fearful of the ocean after what had happened. He said he had found the courage to paddle around close to shore, but he lacked the confidence to catch a wave.

I explained to him that it was a process, that his fearlessness would return in time.

"Basketball has helped me to find my way back," he said. "Without it, I'd be lost."

That reminded me of the way I had felt about the game for so many years before I decided to give it up. Hearing Curtis say those words, I was starting to have second thoughts about my own decision. "You said you needed to talk?"

"You heard about Jed Swagerty?"

"He hasn't been at practice for a couple days. I figured he was feeling the ill effects of hanging around Brock Decker too much."

Curtis said he had learned from Stretch that Coach Kincaid had removed Jed from the basketball program for violation of team rules. "Apparently, Coach K caught Swaggy J puffing on unauthorized contraband behind the gym after practice, and he bounced him."

Curtis said that when he found out there was an opening on the roster, he went to see Coach about filling it, because he thought it would speed up his recovery. He also thought he could make a contribution to the team.

"What'd he say?"

"He said, 'Welcome back, bro.'"

Talk about irony. I had gone from playing on the team without my best friends to watching from the bench while they both played on the team without me.

"Did he really call you 'bro'?"

"Yeah, as far as *you* know."

55

The Light Bulb Inside
My Skull Switched On

I took Mr. Shields's observations to heart and made changes in my daily routine, starting with stashing Wade's truck in the carport and leaving it there. I topped up the air in my bike tires, lubed the drive chain, and put a new battery in the headlamp. I started eating better and drinking more water. I even got my basketball out of the closet and began to take it everywhere I went, just like old times.

At Jefferson, I slipped into the gym every day before practice to work on my perimeter shooting. When my work scheduled allowed, I hung back after practice to run the floor and do ball-handling drills. I spent my weekends at the rec center reconnecting with old friends and playing three-on-three until the sun went down. After a few weeks, I was feeling more like my old self again.

Reconnecting with friends meant checking in with Lawrence. I hadn't seen the math whiz since my dad drove him home after our aborted trip to Kansas. I got on my bike on a Saturday afternoon and rode to his house to see how he was doing. Lawrence's father greeted me at the front door.

"Did Lawrence contact you?"

"No, sir. I haven't spoken with your son in quite awhile."

Mr. Tuckerman told me that Nathan had come over a couple of days before for his weekly chess match with Lawrence, and after Nathan left, Lawrence wouldn't come out of his bedroom. Mr. Tuckerman said he could hear Lawrence pacing and obsessing day and night, muttering something about "calling Zeke," but I never received a phone call.

"I was about to phone you to ask if you could come over and speak with my son."

I walked down the hallway and knocked on Lawrence's door. I heard shuffling inside, but there was no answer.

"Hey, buddy. It's me, Zeke. How's it going in there?"

It all happened so fast: The lock flipped. The door flew open. The hand darted out. *Smack!*

Lawrence had cracked me across the face. The pain waited for a microsecond, no doubt to gather up surrounding pain reinforcements, before engulfing my skin full force. I felt hot blood rushing to that usual spot where people seemed to want to strike me.

Lawrence slammed the door, but he didn't lock it.

"Why can't you just say, 'It's been a long time since you stopped by!'"

I heard the sound of scribbling. Lawrence shoved a folded-up sheet of paper under the door. I picked it up and gave it a quick scan.

Nice of you to stop by.

I pushed open the door and went inside. I could tell that Lawrence had only barricaded himself inside for a day or two, because the impenetrable fog of Lawrence Tuckerman brainpower engulfed just three of my five senses, and my eyes were only watering a little.

I threw open the lone window and stood at the opposite end of the room, well out of striking distance.

"Your dad says you've been meaning to call me. What's up?"

Lawrence wrote another brief note and tore it from his pad. He folded it in half and handed it to me.

Calling!

This was going to take longer than I had thought. "No need to do that. I'm already here."

Another deep sigh from Lawrence fueled a follow-up note.

Nathan said you quit basketball.

So that's what this was about. "Yeah, Nathan was right. I took some time off, but I'm starting to play again."

My response seemed to agitate Lawrence even more. He wrote out a longer note while I pondered whether there might be a secret method of ushering fresh air into the chamber of thickness any faster. Lawrence handed me the note.

CALLING!
Curtis
Stretch
Wade
Nathan
Lawrence

I didn't know what to make of that one. It looked like a list of people Lawrence intended to reach out to. Curtis and Stretch were easy enough to track down. Wade, not so much. Lawrence would only have to wait until his next chess match with Nathan to sit down and chop it up.

As far as Lawrence calling himself was concerned, I wasn't going to touch that one. I was lost. "You need to help me out here."

Lawrence ripped that piece of paper from my hand. He scrawled more words onto it and shoved it back.

CALLING!
Curtis — surfing
Stretch — criminal justice
Wade — Marine Corps
Nathan — chess
Lawrence — space travel

Lawrence was worked up. It was clear those words were important to him. I tried to figure out why. Then Lawrence scratched out yet another note and held it out.

Zeke — basketball

The light bulb inside my skull switched on.

Lawrence wasn't going to *call* all of us. He was telling me that everyone had a *calling*, the one thing they were put on this Earth to do.

Including me.

Lawrence seemed to know that I understood. He spoke to me for the first time since we had left the gas station. "Can't quit. Basketball is your calling."

56

There Wasn't Anything Left to Talk About

I knew Lawrence was right. I had other hobbies and interests, but basketball was my best chance at fulfillment because it provided the greatest opportunity for a deep connection to people.

I was lucky Wade hadn't been around to see me turn my back on the game, or I never would have heard the end of it.

"Quitting is not an option, marine!" he would have barked. *"Drop and give me fifty!"*

I was grateful to Lawrence for helping me look at my life in a new light. I knew what I had to do next. I bolted through the front door and jumped on my bike. My destination was Jefferson Community College.

The basketball season was set to start in three days with a series of nonconference games against tough opponents. I remembered how Coach Kincaid had gotten ready for the opener last season by making final preparations and drawing up new plays on the weekend prior. Our coach was a creature of habit, so I had a feeling I would find him at the college.

I flew down Chamberlain Drive to the campus and propped my bike against the brick wall next to the PE Building entrance. I rushed down the hallway to the coach's office. The door was open. Coach Kincaid was standing at his desk pulling uniforms out of a cardboard box.

I didn't realize I was out of breath until I tried to speak but was unable to form the words. I tried to pull oxygen into my body with deep breaths, but I couldn't force the air into my lungs fast enough. Next thing I knew, I was flat on my back.

"Goodness, Zeke. Are you all right?" Coach was towering above me with a look of grave concern.

"Tell me what I have to do to play on the team."

"One thing at a time." Coach Kincaid grasped my hand and lifted me off the carpet. He helped me over to the same guest chair that I had soaked with residual rainwater a few weeks earlier.

"I need to play, Coach." I wiped the sweat from my forehead with my jacket sleeve. I was determined not to take no for an answer.

In the time I had known Coach Kincaid, he had always chosen his words carefully, so I knew his response would be brief and to the point. Coach sat down at his desk and moved the box of uniforms to the floor.

"I'm only carrying thirteen players on the roster."

There was no wiggle room in those words. With zero other options, the only thing left to do was go for it. If ever there was a time to channel my inner Wade Archer, this was it. It had worked on Coach once before, so I took another shot.

"Can you make an exception?"

I was hoping Coach Kincaid would light up in amusement, or at least crack a smile, but his expression didn't change.

"The team has thirteen players because the college only has thirteen uniforms. It's been that way for years."

I closed my eyes to process that information. I had learned from my friendship with Lawrence that a math problem might travel down a long and winding road, but the answer to it is always the truth.

Lawrence would have agreed that the numbers did not line up in my favor. What I didn't understand was why thirteen was the limit. Why wasn't it, say, fourteen? What was the big deal about an extra jersey and a pair of gym shorts?

Coach Kincaid provided the Jefferson basketball program history lesson, explaining that during the twenty-five years when Vernon Shields was head coach, he had always carried thirteen players because he thought it was the most efficient number of student-athletes to deal with. Efficiency at Jefferson was vital because equipment budgets at the community college level were nowhere near as high as they were at four-year institutions, such as the University of Kansas.

"Do you see that box over there? Mr. Shields gave it to me when he retired. The same thirteen uniforms are in there, including the one you wore last season."

That last bit of info caused me to swallow hard. There wasn't anything left to talk about. I stood up and thanked Coach for his time. "Guess I'll see you at practice Monday." I hung my head and moped down the hallway toward the exit.

"Wait a second," Coach said as I reached for the door handle.

Coach Kincaid had a habit of holding a brief conversation with me in that hallway. I wondered what was coming. Was he going to tell me to make sure I latched the door properly on my way out?

"I like the dedication you've shown as team manager, and I've noticed you've been working hard to stay in shape."

Coach took a lengthy pause. The only sound I heard in that dark hallway was my heart jackhammering against my ribcage. I stood up straight and threw my shoulders back.

"There's no rule that says you can't work out with the team. Stop by on Monday to pick up a reversible practice jersey. We've got more than thirteen of those."

57

Basketball Was on the Horizon

I spent the rest of the weekend at the rec center working on my outside shooting. Curtis and Stretch stopped by on Sunday to play some three-on-three and offer encouragement, which I was in dire need of after so much time away from the game.

Mom packed an extra cheese sandwich in my lunch on Monday morning so that my energy level would be as high as possible, especially after my decision to put Wade's truck on ice.

I expected my first day back at practice to be bumpy. Except for my two best friends and Brock Decker, most of the rest only knew me as the guy who fetched Brock's water bottle on demand. That meant I would have to earn their respect through hustle and teamwork.

"Bring me a fresh towel at once." Brock was not going to make it any easier for me. Sharing the court with him was a lot like working for Nathan, except that I had exchanged my polo shirt for a reversible scrimmage jersey, and Brock would never do something nice for me, like get his grandmother to custom-bake basketball-themed snacks.

My footwork was clumsy. My shot wasn't falling. The entire practice was a wakeup call, a reminder of how rusty I was and how much work I still had to do before I could find my rhythm. By the time Coach Kincaid blew the final whistle of the afternoon, I was exhausted.

Coach rounded everyone up at center court. Brock stood next to me and tried to make a wisecrack about how thirsty he was, but Curtis stepped between us to calm the waters. "Don't go there, dudes," he said.

Coach set down his clipboard and fixed his eyes on the scoreboard. "Tomorrow at this time, we'll have a pretty good idea of where we stand as a team—and gentlemen, it won't have anything to do with the final score."

Coach Kincaid told us to get a good night's sleep and eat a balanced breakfast in the morning. Stretch's eyes lit up on the breakfast part. Coach ended the practice session by saying a few surprise words about me. "I've asked Zeke to scrimmage with the team for the rest of the season as part of his managerial duties. It's good to have him back on the court."

Most of the guys headed for the locker room. Brock hung back to get in the last word. "Gotta check my contract, dweeb. Pretty sure there's a clause in there that says I don't have to share the court with the water boy."

"Can it, cement-head." Hunger always made Stretch cranky.

The big fella downed a three-pack of energy bars and the contents of his water bottle before packing up his duffel bag. "You guys wanna get a pizza? My dad's giving me an extra-long lunch break today so I can carb up for the season opener."

Curtis bowed out because he had too much homework. Brock wasn't invited, so he didn't go, either. I passed because I was scheduled to work the swing shift at Chip's.

I had little left in the tank by the time I padlocked my bike and walked inside the store. I toughed out those four hours the best I could, spending my time stocking shelves and helping customers while Nathan worked the cash register. We had been on the job together long enough to have evolved into a competent duo. Nathan's hard edge was softening over time, and I became more accepting of those fleeting moments when his management style could be harsh.

After I clocked out, I cruised by the basketball section to pick up a new ball and a package of tube socks. I brought them to Nathan's register.

"Looks like you're getting more court time," Nathan said.

"Coach Kincaid said I could practice with the team for the rest of the season."

"You crack the starting lineup?"

"Not exactly."

I explained to Nathan that the tight budget at Jefferson's athletics department only allowed for thirteen uniforms, all of which were spoken for by players whose commitment to the team had been greater than mine during summer tryouts.

"Want me to speak to the coach? I know some folks in the neighborhood who can *handle* this for you."

Nathan arranging to rough up Coach Kincaid in order to free up a roster spot sounded like an idea that was not fully baked.

"That won't be necessary," I said.

"Suit yourself."

Nathan rang up my purchase. It was a great feeling to be able to pay for my own gear rather than rely on my mom. Nathan gave me what he referred to as the rookie employee discount, which was identical to the regular employee discount, except that it gave him an extra opportunity to call me a rookie.

So, after a tough summer and challenging fall, basketball was on the horizon. And where there was basketball, there was hope.

58

Dude, Let's Take a Look at That Schnoz

I remembered what Coach Kincaid had said about the scoreboard as I stared at it in disbelief after the final horn sounded in the season opener. Coach had told us the day before that there would be little connection between the game's outcome and how well the team performed.

I wasn't so sure he was right.

The visiting team, from Sierra Ridge Community College, controlled the contest at both ends of the court and hammered us by forty-nine points. *FORTY-NINE*. It was the most lopsided loss in the entire history of the men's basketball program at Jefferson.

Stretch took an elbow right in the beezer from a Sierra Ridge defender who was trying to drive him out of bounds on a fast break early in the first half. The big man had to bow out with a bloody nose and just two points and a single rebound.

Curtis was a long way from being the player he had been prior to his surfing accident. He missed every shot he attempted and turned an ankle walking to the bench when Coach Kincaid pulled him in the waning moments.

Brock, starting as point guard, committed eleven turnovers before he picked up a pair of technical fouls for cursing at the refs and was tossed with three minutes to go until halftime.

The rest of the guys didn't play much better. It was a total and complete disaster of epic proportions.

The team was sulking its way to the locker room when a familiar voice cut through the drone of the crowd. "The Jefferson Jackrabbits get pummeled by nearly fifty on their home court in the season opener? Not a great way to kick off the season. Care to comment, Zeke?" Darla Davenport was relentless.

"Shouldn't you be interviewing the coach?"

"I'm looking for the insider perspective. You taught me that, remember?"

All I could think about was getting back to the locker room with the team, but I knew that Darla wouldn't let it go until I gave her a quote for her story.

"I like what I saw out there today. It's only a nonconference game. We're going to keep working hard." I waited while Darla jotted it down in her reporter's notebook. "Anything else?"

"Yeah, what was it like watching a train wreck like that from the bench?"

That one hurt. I knew I could have helped my teammates a lot more if I were wearing a uniform instead of a clip-on tie.

"I'm here to help this team any way I can."

I jogged back to the locker room. My teammates were slumped on the benches, heads in hands. The room felt like everyone's dogs had just been hit by the Sierra Ridge team bus.

Stretch was pressing an icepack against his face. The swelling contorted everything sideways, but it worked to his advantage because it made his face seem not as long as usual.

Curtis's ankle was swollen too, wrapped in a crisscross of elastic bandages and cold packs.

The only bruise Brock had suffered was to his ego.

The room fell silent when Coach Kincaid cleared his throat.

"I like what I saw out there today."

I wondered whether Coach and I had attended the same game. As team statistician, I knew that our opponents had outplayed us in every category except player ejections.

"What did we learn today?" Coach was always asking the good ones.

Brock was first to raise his hand. "That we suck?"

A collective moan of agreement circled the locker room.

"What about you, Zeke? What did you learn today about this team?"

Coach had put me on the spot. I was only the team manager, but I knew in my heart that the outcome would've been different had I been on the court and dressed to play instead of only near it and *over*dressed to *not* play. I also thought Coach Kincaid was looking to me for leadership when it was clear the team needed some.

"I learned that we have a lot of work to do."

That brought out even more groans. Brock flung his towel at me. "Here's some work for you to do. Wash this."

I ignored him and kept going. "We ran the offense. We boxed out on defense. We communicated. We just need to put it all together."

All eyes shifted back to Coach Kincaid. "Zeke's right. I couldn't have asked for more than that." Coach walked over to the chalkboard and wrote two words:

TEAM   WORK

"If we can put those together every day in practice, we'll be fine. It's up to you. Get some rest. Practice starts tomorrow at two o'clock."

Most of the guys hit the showers. Curtis and Stretch hung back. So did I—I had no need for a shower because stat guys never get sweaty enough.

Curtis hobbled over to where Stretch was sitting. "Dude, let's take a look at that schnoz."

"You guys get the license plate number of that elbow driving the Mack truck?" Stretch set down the icepack. His nose looked as if someone had knocked it sideways with a clawhammer and then used a knitting needle to sew a second, more grotesque nose onto the side of it.

Curtis tried to downplay the seriousness of Stretch's injury. "It's not so gnarly, bro. Honest."

I took a more diplomatic approach. "I think it makes you look tougher."

We vowed to work harder in practice before going our separate ways into the night.

Curtis regained his shooting touch over the next couple of months. Stretch grew to seven feet, four inches, and his nose got back to normal pretty fast. Brock even managed to keep his temper in check.

But none of it mattered. The vaunted Jefferson Jackrabbits lost nineteen more games in a row to build a record of 0–20 heading into the start of Southern Region Conference play.

59

The Bitter-Cold Wind Sliced Across My Face

I clocked in for my shift at Chip's.

I stood in the basketball aisle spinning a ball on my index finger as I tried to figure out how the bottom had fallen out of a season that had once held so much promise.

The beginning of Southern Region Conference action was a day away. The only thing that could save the team from itself was a miracle.

"I'm not paying you to wear out that ball." Nathan wasn't the one signing my paychecks, but his point was well taken.

"I was performing a routine quality check. This ball is approved for retail purchase."

Nathan handed me a laundry list of the duties he needed me to handle, which included restocking the entire store. I welcomed the extra responsibility because I needed something to take my mind off the tremendous shame I was feeling over losing my roster spot.

The level of competition in conference games would be greater. No doubt the remainder of the season would plummet deeper into the vortex of failure. I was powerless to do anything beyond making sure my teammates were well hydrated as they got creamed in the final eight games of the regular season, plus documenting the statistics of our wretched failure.

Nathan seized the opportunity to give me something extra to worry about for the next four hours.

"Boss wants to see you before you go home."

"What's it about?"

"I don't know, but chances are it's not good. It might have something to do with you wearing out the store's inventory of basketballs."

I spent the rest of my shift wondering whether Chip was going to fire me. On the bright side, if he did, I would have more free time to feel sorry for myself.

The basketball section was the easiest to restock because I knew exactly where Chip kept that equipment in the storage room.

The chess and checkers section was a cinch too. It was small, and there wasn't much to do over there because Nathan took great pride in making sure the game boards, strategy books, and score sheets were always fully stocked and organized.

After that, I hand-trucked merchandise to the football, baseball, and soccer sections, where Chip did the majority of his business.

I stopped cold in my tracks for a moment as I wheeled over to the rugby section. I thought about how the drop-kick kid had remained a baffling mystery, there one moment and gone the next. I spent the next several minutes tidying up the rugby shelves while looking over my shoulder, halfway thinking the kid might materialize to taunt me before disappearing again.

I crossed the last item off Nathan's list and trudged to the back of the store to clock out, grab my backpack, and find out from Chip how much worse my day would get before my head hit the pillow.

Chip's nose was buried in a stack of papers. "You look tired," he said.

"Yes, sir."

"How's Nathan treating you?"

I wasn't sure if that was a trick question. Nathan pushed me to the limit, but most of the time it was for the good of the store and its customers.

"Best boss I ever had."

Chip seemed to stifle a grin. He knew the job there was my first ever, so I didn't have former supervisors to compare against Nathan.

"I like his focus," Chip said. "The chess and checkers gear has never been so well organized."

Chip rummaged through a soaring pile of stuff in the corner of his office. He pulled out a small package and tossed it across his desk.

"I need to get that to Coach Kincaid tomorrow, but I don't have time to stop by the college."

I stuffed it into my backpack. "On it, boss."

I unlocked my bike and smacked the kickstand with my sneaker. Riding home to my apartment at night had become a ritual form of meditation, a time to dwell on my dead brother, my former girlfriend, and my broken basketball season.

I strapped on my helmet and retraced a path across the congested asphalt arteries that defined my life in Los Angeles.

The bitter-cold wind sliced across my face as I contemplated whether anyone behind the wheel of a car hurtling past me was carrying a burden as heavy as mine.

60

My Heart Froze and Then Started Pounding

The Jackrabbits' conference opener was a home game. I drifted through the school day biding my time until journalism, my last class before stats-and-water detail at the arena.

I knew we would be laying out pages for the upcoming edition of the *Jefferson Journal*, which was scheduled for publication the next morning. Ace sports reporter Darla Davenport greeted me at the door, reporter's notebook in hand.

"What are the chances of the team extending its losing streak to twenty-one in a row today?"

"Not now, Darla."

"C'mon, I need some copy. I've set aside six columns above the fold on the Sports front for my gamer."

Darla was using her best newsroom insider jargon. Translation: she planned to write a lengthy story about the game's unfavorable outcome, and she had designed the Sports section so there would be ample space for coverage of the carnage.

After class, I hauled butt to the locker room so I could use the mirror there to put on my clip-on tie. The guys were already in uniform when I arrived. I sat down in front of what used to be my locker.

Coach Kincaid hadn't named a team captain because no one had yet stepped forward in a leadership role. That meant the mood in there was drifting from glum to dismal as tipoff approached.

Brock was carrying out his usual pregame ritual of reading a comic book. Rodrigo and Chen, two of the team's freshmen, were doing homework.

Stretch was forcing a folded-up slice of pizza through the narrow mouth hole of the full-face plastic mask he now wore to protect his nose from any further errant elbows. I could tell he was trying to act like that looked normal.

"I'm thinking of wearing this as a disguise when I'm working undercover," he said.

Curtis was sipping a cup of green tea. He walked over and leaned in. "Does Stretch's mask make me look fat?" he whispered.

I admired my friends for finding ways to make the best of a challenging situation.

I reached into my backpack for my clip-on tie and noticed the package Chip had asked me to deliver to Coach Kincaid. Hassling the clip-on would have to wait. I walked down the

PE Department hallway to the coach's office and went inside. Coach was sitting at his desk sketching out random X's and O's on a chalkboard.

"Pencil sharpener's over there," he said.

"Chip Spears asked me to deliver this to you." I handed Coach Kincaid the package.

Coach stood up from his chair. "Tell Chip I said thanks."

I left the coach's office and headed back down the hallway to hang out with the guys until the game got underway. I was about to turn the door handle when I heard Coach Kincaid's voice cut through the silence. By that time, it was clear he was a big fan of the head coach–team manager hallway conversation. "I think this is for you."

I retraced my steps back to the coach's office. Coach Kincaid returned the package to me. I opened it.

Inside I found a hunter-green basketball jersey and a matching pair of gold trunks with green piping. The number 14 was stitched onto the front and back of the jersey.

My heart froze and then started pounding.

I looked up at Coach in disbelief. "I don't understand."

"Apparently, a coworker of yours, someone named Nathan Freeman, told Chip Spears that the basketball team wasn't budgeted for a fourteenth player. Chip had a meeting with Jefferson's athletic director and worked out a sponsorship deal that includes a fourteenth uniform."

That uniform felt like a pair of silk pajamas in my hands. "I don't know what to say, Coach."

"Better suit up. Conference opener starts in thirty minutes."

61

Then a Funny Thing Happened

I went back to the locker room and changed into my new uniform without saying a word to anyone. It was a perfect fit. All eyes were on me. Luckily, I always wore my favorite court sneakers in my managerial role, the faster to fetch water and towels for the other guys.

Brock Decker saw what I was doing and counted out loud the number of players in the room. "Fourteen. We're all here," he said. "It appears you didn't roll one of us in the parking lot to get that."

I explained to my teammates that the college had amended its policy of limiting the roster to thirteen players. I sensed a collective sigh of relief as I received high fives from everyone, including cement-head himself.

A minute later, Coach Kincaid came into the locker room.

"I've asked Zeke to join the team for the rest of the campaign. He's worked hard in practice and as team manager, so I think it's only fair for him to share the court with us."

After that, Coach set the starting lineup: Stretch at center, Rodrigo and Chen as the forwards, Curtis as shooting guard, and Brock at the point.

"Bring it in, fellas," Coach finished.

The team let loose with a collective cheer and streamed onto the court for pregame warmups. When Darla Davenport saw me in uniform doing layup drills with the team, she waved Stretch over to the sideline.

"It's been a long time since Zeke played competitive basketball at this level," Darla said within earshot of me. "Are you worried he's not ready?"

"Zeke Archer was born ready," Stretch replied. "You just worry about spelling my name right after we torch these guys—there are two *t*'s in Puckett."

Stretch's contentious encounter with a member of the press corps seemed to increase his energy level. The big man went up high to control the opening tip, and that led to an easy layup and an early lead.

But North Los Angeles College was talented and had a deep bench. It wasn't long before our opponent took control of the momentum and surged ahead, taking a fifteen-point lead at the half.

Coach Kincaid paced up and down the locker room while the guys caught their breath and settled in. Coach picked up a stick of chalk and drew the same two words onto the blackboard that he had written after we got slaughtered by Sierra Ridge in the season opener:

TEAM   WORK

"Box out, make good outlet passes, run the break like we practiced," Coach said. "We're in better shape than these guys. Let's run them off the court!"

That was all the team needed to hear. Brock took over in the second half, driving up the tempo and directing traffic for layup after easy layup. The Jackrabbits regained the lead midway through the second half and cruised to an easy victory, the team's first of the season. I even got some playing time when Coach subbed me in for Brock during garbage time in the closing minutes.

If it weren't for Nathan, I never would've had the chance to play that season. The next day at work, I thanked him for his friendship and for standing up for me with the boss.

"Don't go all soft on me, rookie, or I'll have to write you up."

For the next two weeks, I juggled my time between schoolwork, my part-time job at Chip's, and the basketball team.

The sporting goods store's sponsorship deal with Jefferson was a signature Chip Spears win-win business decision that paid immediate dividends. I noticed an influx of college students coming into the store to purchase gear.

I picked up more and more playing time each game until I was splitting point guard duties with Brock right down the middle. Brock appeared to be annoyed about having to share the backcourt, but I think he secretly enjoyed our revitalized friendship.

The crowds grew larger and more boisterous with each successive Jackrabbits victory. My mom was able to take off enough time from her responsibilities at the hospital to attend home games. Dad even called one night to say he planned to drive to Los Angeles to attend a playoff game if we made it to the postseason.

Despite our crappy start in nonconference play, we ran the table, winning all seven of our remaining regular-season games to take the Southern Region Conference title. Even though the Jackrabbits had a losing overall record of 8–20, our unblemished conference play was enough to send us headlong into the regional playoffs.

Then a funny thing happened.

We knocked off teams from Eastern Hills Community College and Valley Tech to earn a berth in the Southern California Regional Championship game.

It would be a rematch against our crosstown rival, Westside City College, the team that had edged us out by a single point at the buzzer in the regional finals exactly one year earlier.

Finally, our improbable shot at redemption had come.

62

I Was Wrong

I clocked out at Chip's and waved goodbye to Nathan. The big game for all the marbles was two nights away. I was looking forward to the bike ride home because it was a chance to relax and collect my thoughts.

When I had called my dad earlier in the day to give him the news about the team's success, he told me he was going to drive in from Denver for the title game. My mom had already arranged to take the night off from work. I knew they might sit together in the bleachers, so we would have a fleeting chance to be three-quarters of a family again for a couple of hours.

I figured there would be a lot of other people at the game who had all played a role in my success on the court. No doubt Chip Spears would be there. So would rec center director Vernon Shields. Heck, I thought Chett Biffmann might even drop by.

"It's kind of late for you to be riding around on that confounded bicycle," Mrs. Fenner said as I pulled up to my apartment building.

"Yes, Mrs. Fenner. Thank you for noticing."

Then Mrs. Fenner caught me by surprise. "Good luck in the big match on Saturday. I hope you score a lot of runs."

I gave Mrs. Fenner partial credit for at least knowing there was an important game on the horizon, and I dragged my bike up the stairs.

When I walked inside my apartment, I saw my mom standing in the kitchen, still in her hospital scrubs and on the phone. She was doing a whole lot of listening, but not much talking. I had a bad feeling about the conversation she was having.

Mom hung up and turned on the burner under the teapot. I could tell she was avoiding me, so I went to my bedroom without saying anything.

A few minutes later, she walked in.

"That was the California Highway Patrol. There's been an incident."

Mom said the authorities had found Dad's pickup truck parked along southbound Interstate 15 on the side of the highway near Victorville. The headlamps were on and the engine was idling. The CHP officer found my dad inside the cab staring off into space.

"Your father was driving in for the championship game. I think he had an emotional breakdown. I guess he finally ran out of steam."

After all the tears my mom had shed for Wade, I didn't think she could have any left for my dad.

I was wrong.

63

Always Go Strong to the Rack, Right?

Just when it felt like my life was getting back on track, the bottom had fallen out again.

The CHP took my dad to a hospital in Victorville for diagnosis. Once hospital authorities determined he wasn't a threat to anyone but himself, the Veterans Administration moved him to the West Los Angeles VA Medical Center for observation and treatment.

I loved my father, but I felt that I didn't really know him. Our relationship had changed when my parents divorced and he moved to Denver. After that, I didn't hear from him for months at a time. At one point, he sent me a letter to explain why he had disappeared. He wrote about the terrible things he had witnessed while serving in the army during the Iraq

War, including the deaths of innocent civilians. Many were women and children who lost their lives in his presence.

"War is hell," he used to tell me. My dad knew because he had lived it.

Curtis and Stretch were there for me, just as they had been when Wade was killed in action. Even Brock was being less of a tool than usual. It was not easy focusing on the title game, but there was no way I would let down my teammates again.

On game day, I rode my bike to Jefferson and arrived four hours before tipoff. I wanted to give myself ample time to square my head and stuff the pain deep down where it wouldn't get in my way. I was alone in the locker room when Coach Kincaid poked his head in the door.

"How are you doing, son?"

"I've been better, Coach."

Coach took a seat on the opposite side of the room and looked around at the lockers and shower stalls. He seemed to be sizing up the moment.

"Tonight's game doesn't mean much. It's just a game."

"If you say so." I had no idea what Coach Kincaid was talking about. The chance to win the regional championship was the most important thing in my life—ever. If Coach was trying to make me feel better, it wasn't working.

"The game is only of consequence in the moment it's taking place," he said. "That's why there's beauty in playing the game to the absolute best of your ability. We only have the moment we're in."

Curtis had once spoken of living in the moment when he learned about something called existentialism in his philosophy class. He said it meant he had the freedom to determine his own life path through authentic choices and acts of free will. I figured Coach Kincaid was telling me the same thing.

"I think I understand, Coach. Always go strong to the rack, right?"

"Something like that."

My conversation with Coach Kincaid helped put me in a better frame of mind. By the time my teammates arrived, I felt ready to take on our opponents. Coach offered final words of instruction and announced the customary starting lineup of Curtis and Stretch, Rodrigo and Chen, and Brock.

Just when I thought Coach had no more surprises up his sleeve, he appointed team captains for the final game of the year.

Brock.

And me.

Stretch added the final battle cry before we took the floor in front of a raucous crowd: "Let's go get us some hardware!"

64

The Answers on That Night Would Have to Come from Within

Stretch nearly leaped through the roof of the gym to control the opening tip to Brock, who whipped a two-handed chest pass to Curtis in stride for a deep three-pointer and an early lead.

Westside's shooting guard countered with a three-ball of his own, setting the tone for a seesaw battle between two evenly matched and equally hungry teams.

Stretch's skyhook was finding its mark, and he hounded the glass with authority on both ends. Curtis had regained his deadly shooting touch from downtown. Rodrigo and Chen called out the picks and played lockdown defense.

Coach Kincaid rotated Brock and me at point guard to keep us fresh—a keen strategy because I could go all out on the court and then catch my breath on the bench before Coach tapped me in again. I sensed that Brock didn't like being subbed out, but Coach stuck to his game plan, and Brock didn't have much to say about it.

The game's high stakes heightened the energy level on the court in the first half. The game grew more physical and contentious with every possession, ramping up the provocative language and hard shoving that the referees struggled to control.

Westside hit a buzzer-beating trey to take a 39–38 advantage into the locker room at the break.

Curtis sat on the floor cross-legged and set down his headband. He closed his eyes and ran a hand through his wet hair to draw his focus inward.

Stretch had his own take on inward focus. He peeled off his mask and pulled a cold double-cheeseburger and soggy fries from his locker. "Anyone got any ketchup?"

Brock was practicing proper halftime nutrition with a bag of spicy pork rinds and a twenty-four-ounce energy drink.

Coach Kincaid wheeled the blackboard to the center of the locker room. By that point in a long season, his stick of chalk was little more than a tiny nub. He picked it up and scratched out a simple message on the board:

100%

Coach made eye contact with every player on the team.

"I'd like each one of you, from the starters to the third string, to consider giving your teammates one-hundred percent effort in the second half," Coach said. "If you do, we'll always know we gave it everything we had, win or lose."

One by one across the locker room, my teammates, each in his own way, acknowledged Coach's words.

For Coach Kincaid, at the moment, the wheel had come full circle. He had been in the crowd at the Jefferson gymnasium that fateful night two years earlier when Brock and I touched off a near riot at the high school city finals. In an instant, my momentary lapse of judgment set my life on a rocky course filled with heartache and loss.

Coach had been there for Brock and me as we rebuilt our lives. Most of it had little to do with basketball. Coach seemed to know it was time to step aside and let us figure it out for ourselves.

"Captains, this is your team," he said. "I'll see you out there."

With that, Coach Kincaid turned and walked out of the locker room, leaving the team in Brock's hands and mine. The guys sat in stunned silence. The answers on that night would have to come from within.

Stretch stepped forward to break the silence. Even though he wasn't a co-captain, he took it upon himself to sharpen the team's focus.

"We've still got a few minutes before the second half. You think there's any ketchup in Coach's office?"

65

We'll Win It in Overtime

We had fallen behind by a dozen points early in the second half when Brock lost it, slamming his Westside opponent to the hardwood to keep him from scoring on a breakaway layup. The referee blasted his whistle and pointed at Brock.

"Foul! Flagrant one! Number forty!"

Coach Kincaid called a timeout to settle us down.

"Guy had it coming," Brock said as he stood in the huddle fuming.

We had come too far to let the game slip through our fingers because one of our guys was having a meltdown. Curtis stepped in front of Brock, moving so close that their noses were almost touching.

"Only gonna say this once, bro. Pull it together, *now*."

"Get outta my face, surfer boy!"

Coach Kincaid swiveled his head toward me. His unspoken message: *What are you going to do about it, team captain?*

I wedged my body between Brock and Curtis to separate them. The rest of the guys looked at me, wondering what I would say.

"I promise to sign us up for group therapy after we win this thing," I said.

"They serve food at those meetings?" I didn't know how serious Stretch was about his question, but we managed to get Curtis and Brock to take a step back. The game got underway again without any punches thrown.

Brock and I picked up the pace on offense, driving the ball downcourt on fast breaks whenever Stretch grabbed a rebound and fired off an outlet pass. We had trimmed Westside's lead to three points, with two minutes left to play, when I hit Chen with a bounce pass on the break. Chen's Westside defender clotheslined him, sending Chen sprawling to the floor and the ball flying out of bounds.

When the defender stood over Chen and taunted him, both coaches and all three referees rushed over to head off a brawl.

"Technical foul!"

Out of the corner of my eye, I saw Brock leap off the bench. There was fire in his eyes as he marched directly toward the altercation. I intercepted him before he could get far and dragged him back to the bench.

"Get off me!"

"Knock it off!" I bellowed back.

"That chump takes a cheap shot at one of your teammates, and you're just going to stand there?"

Brock must have been suffering from temporary amnesia. That exact play had occurred two years earlier at the high school finals, when Brock was the star point guard at Mid-City Prep and I was captain of Southland Central: a cheap shot followed by a free-for-all. Then we were both expelled, and I kissed my scholarship to the University of Kansas goodbye.

"Any of this look familiar to you?"

Brock blinked and stared at the mass of humanity jostling under the basket. The light inside his thick cement-head seemed to go on.

"Yeah, I get it, but you're still a dweeb."

"Good, 'cause you're still a blockhead."

The refs hadn't seen Brock leave the bench. If they had, he would've been tossed for sure.

Chen nailed both free throws plus an additional one for the technical foul. That tied it at 77–77, but it appeared Chen had suffered an injury on the play. Coach Kincaid called another timeout to get him to the bench.

"Brock, you're in," Coach Kincaid said. "Zeke, you're running the point."

The score remained knotted as both teams went cold in the closing moments of the second half. When Brock bounced the ball off his foot and out of bounds with twenty-five seconds left in regulation, Coach Kincaid called our final timeout.

Coach was calm. The rest of us were anything but.

"We've got these guys exactly where we want them," Coach said. "We're out of timeouts. It doesn't matter if they score. Either way, they're going to press. Punch through it and run the break."

Curtis backed away from the huddle. He unlaced his high-tops and kicked them off. Then he peeled off his socks.

"What are you doing?" Stretch said.

"Way too much traction, bro. Going with my trusty deck shoes."

Stretch seemed to be caught up in the moment. He ripped the protective mask from his face and slammed it down on the bench. "Let's do this!"

Coach Kincaid issued his final instructions. "Man-to-man defense. If they hit a three, push the ball down court and get it to Curtis. If we're down by a bucket, we don't need a three-pointer. Let's just tie it up. We'll win it in overtime."

66

I Hit the Brakes and Sized Up My Options

The culmination of my entire basketball career—from park league to Southland Central High to Jefferson Community College—had come down to twenty-five precious ticks of the clock. By that point in the regional final, I was dead tired and running on hope and adrenaline.

The crowd rose to its feet. Win or lose, I would live in the moment and be ready to accept the outcome.

Curtis and Stretch, Rodrigo, Brock, and I set up on defense.

Rodrigo barked out a reminder. "Call the picks!"

The referee blew his whistle. A Westside player inbounded the ball to the team's point guard. I chased him around the backcourt trying for the steal, but he was too quick and eluded me. He crossed the midcourt stripe just ahead of a ten-second violation.

I was doing everything I knew how to keep him from maneuvering within striking distance. I glanced at the scoreboard. Twelve seconds left. We just needed to hang on to get it to OT.

My man was tattooing the dribble and grinding down the clock. Then all at once, he jab-faked to his right and crossed over to his left. I backpedaled to keep him in front of me, but he ran me hard into a screen.

Brock hadn't called out the pick. I never saw it coming.

My opponent pounded a one-bounce dribble with his left hand to steady himself, then transferred the ball to his right and fired off an unguarded eighteen-foot jumper.

Swish.

My heart sank. Now we were down by a bucket, 79–77. When the crowd roared, I felt the hardwood vibrating beneath my feet like an earthquake. I looked up at the clock. Seven seconds left in the season. We had no timeouts left.

The ref flipped the basketball to Stretch for the inbound pass.

Brock was waving for the ball, but Stretch found me open in the corner. Three Westside defenders swarmed over and trapped me there.

I couldn't see any of my teammates. I was desperate. I threw a sharp head fake, hoping to evade the trio. There was a sliver of daylight. I bolted through it and drove the leather toward the rack in a race against time.

When I crossed half court, I was picked up by two defenders. Curtis appeared in my field of vision, rocketing down the hardwood to my right. Stretch, his long, skinny legs pumping away with everything he had, caught up with us and filled the lane on my left.

Over my shoulder, I caught a glimpse of Brock trailing the play. I eyeballed the clock as I approached the top of the key. Five seconds left.

Everything around me was unfolding in a swirling, flawless rhythm. I was running *the play* to *perfection*.

When I arrived at the free-throw line with three seconds to go, I hit the brakes and sized up my options.

Then it happened again.

For the third time.

67

I Wondered Where the Basketball Had Gone

Pitch black. Total silence.

Please, not again.

By that point, I was used to it, another in a series of perfectly executed fast breaks that transported me through a top-secret interdimensional elevator shaft to heaven-knows-where.

Had I fallen into some supernatural distortion of reality that existed at the precipice of time and space?

Maybe I had been shuttled to another planet. Or beamed to a distant galaxy. Or tossed into a parallel universe.

Or maybe running the fast break with the So-Cal championship on the line was too much for my weary body, and I had suffered a heart attack and died fifteen feet from victory.

I blinked. The smallest sliver of light from above illuminated the floor beneath my feet.

I was standing on a basketball court.

Relief.

The ball was no longer in my hands.

Terror.

The muscles in my arms and legs tightened. When more light filtered in, I realized I was in the middle of a dense, billowing fog. I was barely able to see my hands in front of my face.

"Hello, butt."

I knew that voice. It was the drop-kick kid, William Webb Ellis. What was *he* doing here?

William Webb Ellis materialized through the mist right before my eyes. He was wearing the same leather boots, baggy trousers, and bow tie he had on when he kick-slammed the ball through the basket, rugby-style, after I air-balled the potential game-winner at the regional finals my freshman season.

I was unable to stop my clammy hands from shaking.

"Ellis, William Webb—at your service. Nothing to be afraid of."

"Where am I?"

"Dandy fine question, I'd say."

My mind flashed back to the sports history book I had checked out of the public library years earlier. The book contained a chapter on how a small faction of rugby historians believed that the game was invented by a schoolboy named

William Webb Ellis in 1823 in the Midlands of central England.

Possible. When the drop-kick kid showed up at Wade's funeral, Rebecca did peg his accent as Welsh, not English.

"I'm not an expert on dialects of the United Kingdom like my former girlfriend, but there's something weird about your accent."

"A bit of trickery, I'm afraid. The Entity grants me certain leeway to carry out my mission."

"What mission?"

"In due time, Ezekiel."

William Webb Ellis explained that the 7th Dimension had forbidden him from giving away his identity until the time was right, so he had disguised his voice.

"If I used my native English Midlands accent, or more specifically, my Warwickshire regional subdialect, you would've been on to me for sure."

The fog grew thicker in direct proportion to my rising level of confusion and fear.

"I suppose this is all going to lead somewhere, like what your mission is?"

"Are you familiar with the relationship between rugby and basketball?"

An excellent stall tactic by William Webb Ellis, answering my question with an intriguing one of his own.

The sports history book asserted that Dr. Naismith had drawn elements from football, soccer, lacrosse, and rugby when he invented basketball in 1891, nearly seventy years after the birth of rugby.

"The good doctor had a soft spot in his heart for me because of my direct link to his creation. Decades later, when I got in some hot water with the Entity, he stood up for me and offered to take me under his wing."

That was fascinating sports history, but it still didn't explain what William Webb Ellis's mission was. I wondered where the basketball had gone and whether anyone at Jefferson was concerned about my sudden disappearance. I was losing my patience.

"Please just tell me what your damn mission is!"

"I look after people," he said. "I was supposed to look after Wade, but I made a bit of a mess out of that one, so I promised to square it with the Entity by making sure you arrived here safely."

"What in the world are you talking about?"

I was startled by a thunderous *clank-thunk!* that rattled my eardrums and echoed across the dark, empty spaces above. It was followed by the sound of heavy machinery rumbling to life. The air around me stirred and shifted.

Then the English schoolboy from the early nineteenth century, the young lad who had identified himself as guardian angel William Webb Ellis, evaporated along with the lingering fog, right before my eyes.

68

Thump-Thump-Thump— Whoosh!

My surroundings were in clear view. I was at the ground-level entrance of a cold and cavernous basketball arena, one that was a whole lot bigger than the Jefferson gym. That metallic clamor must have been the facility's ventilation system kicking on and pulling out the fog.

I had a strange feeling that I had been here before. There were alternating aisles of blue, red, and gold seats. High up on the other side of the building there were two rows of jerseys that looked as though they were on display to honor players whose numbers had been retired. Above them I saw an American flag, a Kansas state flag, and a blue-and-white flag with an enormous red K in the center.

There was a painting of a gigantic bird on the hardwood at center court. I knew that bird! It was the Kansas Jayhawk, KU's mythical avian mascot.

I was standing in Allen Fieldhouse, the mecca of college basketball.

Memories came flooding back of the Western Regional three-on-three basketball tournament there a year earlier. Curtis, Stretch, and I had lost a heartbreaker in the finals to the Future Jayhawks, three local high school phenoms who went on to play for the University of Kansas.

Following the awards ceremony, KU head coach Bob Worth offered me a chance to try out for the team as a walk-on after the university rescinded my all-expenses-paid education months earlier.

"No scholarship in the first year. No promises, either. Just an opportunity to come to Lawrence, Kansas, and prove yourself," Coach Worth had told me at the time. I had turned down his offer. It seemed like a lifetime ago.

In the rafters behind me were five national championship banners, from 1922, 1923, 1952, 1988, and 2008. Above them was a sign waving in the breeze: PAY HEED, ALL WHO ENTER: BEWARE OF "THE PHOG."

I understood the *pay heed* part. I was standing there shaking in my high-tops and paying a ton of heed because I was scared out of my mind.

The Phog symbolism wasn't lost on me, either. *Fog* was spelled that way because the arena was named after legendary coach Forrest Clare "Phog" Allen, who had piloted the KU men's basketball program for nearly four decades. He was a disciple of Dr. Naismith and an ethereal presence in the building. Phog Allen acquired the nickname because of the unique foghorn voice he was purported to have had while umpiring behind the plate at baseball games.

It had to be a dream. How was it possible that I had been plucked from Jefferson with the game on the line and deposited at a place most people considered to be the epicenter of college basketball?

I squeezed my eyes shut. I thought that maybe when I opened them, I would somehow be transported back to the Jefferson gym. I heard a leathery *thump-thump-thump—whoosh!* coming from somewhere on the court.

I opened my eyes and saw a man at the basket on the other side of the arena shooting free throws.

Thump-thump-thump—whoosh!

I stepped onto the court and eased my way toward him. I felt my lips trembling and the hair lifting off my arms. I was petrified.

Whoever was shooting, he sure had excellent form—knee, elbow, wrist, all in perfect alignment.

As I got closer, I noticed that the man was wearing a basketball uniform with the number 7 stitched onto the back of his jersey.

Thump-thump-thump—whoosh!

When I got to within a few feet of him, he turned around. It was my brother.

69

Destiny Awaits

Next thing I knew, I was flat on my back on the hardwood. I must have had a panic attack and passed out
from fear. It was the only conceivable explanation I could
think of, because Wade was dead and buried, six feet under at
Southland Meadows Memorial Park.

When I opened my eyes, a hand was reaching down in
front of my face. I grabbed ahold of it. Whoever owned that
hand pulled me to my feet.

I gulped and focused on the person standing before me.

"I'm kinda surprised to see you here, little brother. I heard
you quit basketball."

Warm tears rolled down my cheeks as I hugged my
brother for the first time since he had surprised me by showing up at Allen Fieldhouse a year earlier for the three-on-
three tourney.

"Better let go. We don't have much time."

"I thought you were dead."

"Sorry about the dramatic entrance. I thought it was a bit over the top, but the folks who run this operation have their rules."

I had a million questions for Wade, starting with who had been in the casket that cemetery workers lowered into the ground at Southland Meadows.

"You need to listen carefully to everything I say. I can only say it once, then I have to go."

I knew better than to not listen to my big brother. I stood at attention and obeyed his instructions.

"Remember what Dr. Naismith told you before he died, about how physical death is not the end of consciousness, because all consciousness is infinite and without beginning or end?"

"Sort of." All I remembered was how scared I was and how the doctor's words seemed like total gibberish. And how did Wade know what Dr. Naismith had said to me, anyway?

Wade backed up Dr. Naismith's words. "Free will allows people who are near death to have one last chance to communicate with someone of their choosing before they cross over to the other side."

"This is freaking me out," I said, shivering with fear. "Is any of this real, or just a bad dream?"

"Funny you should ask. Most last-chance encounters happen in the dream state, but I asked the Entity to create a fast-break portal because I knew it was the best way for us to connect."

The only reason I believed any of this was because it was coming from my brother.

"I tried the first time at the regional finals last year, but you weren't ready," Wade said. "The second time, in the fighting hole in Afghanistan, you were ready, but I wasn't. So, I asked for an exception."

To the best of my knowledge, Wade was the first person in civilized society to ever ask for an exception. He had once explained that it was okay to ask for one, but you had better have a darned good reason for asking, or the request would likely be denied.

Then Wade told me that Lawrence's theory about human consciousness surviving death was true.

"Lawrence learned from the 7th Dimension that our bodies are made from the same basic materials as everything that exists in the universe. Human consciousness is what interconnects it all, from unexplained phenomena to alternate-reality contact experiences with nonhuman intelligence."

That made my head hurt. "I'm not sure I know what that means."

"We don't have much time left. Let me break it down for you this way." Wade held the ball up with both hands. "Imagine this basketball is the universe."

Since basketball was already my universe and the prism through which I viewed my world, I felt confident that I would understand the explanation to follow.

"The air inside the ball collectively comprises all consciousness that exists in the universe. It's all working together to support the ball so that it can bounce perfectly on the court."

Wade let go of the ball. It hit the wood floor and bounced straight and true, right back into his waiting hands.

"I must go now. Destiny awaits."

What? We were just getting started. There was so much more to talk about. "Where are you going?"

"Home, little buddy. I'm going home."

That empty feeling of loss was consuming me all over again. Wade seemed to notice and tried his best to comfort me.

"Remember in my letter, when I said I'd send you a sign when I got to where I was going? I found out it's not standard procedure to do that, because the universe's system is faith-based." Then Wade flashed a toothy grin, and I saw in his eyes what I can only describe as divine light. "That won't stop me from asking for an exception, though."

Wade threw me a two-handed bounce pass. In the space of time that the ball traveled between us, he said these simple words: "You are the air in the basketball. You are part of something bigger."

When the ball hit my hands, Allen Fieldhouse went black.

70

Time Seemed to Stand Still

I blinked and focused my eyes. I was planted at the free-throw line, fifteen feet from the title.

I wanted to dwell on what had just happened at Allen Fieldhouse, but there was no time. I needed to deal with the basketball business at hand. I had three seconds in which to do it.

If I could get the ball to Curtis, he was money. But his defender was covering him like a thick fog. I had no chance.

The guy guarding Stretch was also a seven-footer. He ran Stretch off the play with a subtle body check. Then that same defender came right at me, his long arms lifting toward the ceiling.

Two seconds left. I was down to a couple of options. Neither was very good. I could force up a high-arch prayer over the defender, or somehow get the ball to Brock Decker—who had trailed the play as the safety valve—for an even bigger prayer.

I bent my knees and elevated for a jumper. As I hung in midair, my gut told my brain that the behemoth defender with arms like goalposts would surely swat my shot.

Final option: Plan B.

I was inches from touching the floor again when I rifled a no-look, behind-the-back bounce pass to where I thought Brock would be standing. The ball skipped off the hardwood and hit Brock square in his wheelhouse. The ball even landed logo-side up.

Brock glanced down at the three-point line and saw that he was standing on it. Disregarding Coach Kincaid's instructions to go for the tie to get the game into overtime, he took a one-bounce dribble and stepped back behind the arc.

Then he launched a three-pointer that exited his hand a fraction of a second before the final horn sounded.

Time seemed to stand still as Brock's shot defied gravity before it plummeted back down to earth. It slammed hard off the heel of the basket, bounced about seven feet straight up in the air, and floated back down through the center of the net.

Swish—sort of.

80–79.

Ballgame.

71

I Can Make You One
Helluva Deal

The shot was reminiscent of a nearly identical one that Wade had once told me about. It was made by Boston Celtics small forward Don Nelson, who knocked down a back-rim masterpiece in the 1969 NBA Finals to help the Celts defeat Wade's favorite team, the Los Angeles Lakers.

Our entire team dogpiled on top of Brock. I dropped to my knees and wept, face down, atop the Jackrabbit mascot painted onto the hardwood at center court.

It was the championship I had worked for my entire life, but it felt hollow because my brother and father weren't there to witness it.

I felt a tap on my back. When I rolled over, there was a hand reaching down in front of my face. I grabbed ahold of it. The hand's owner pulled me to my feet.

"What took you so long, dweeb? I couldn't have been more wide open if the gym was empty."

"Nice shot, cement-head," I replied. "Way to use the rim."

Curtis and Stretch joined us for a round of hugs and high fives. I even hugged Brock. Or maybe he hugged me, I don't know.

Mom was the first to come down from the bleachers and congratulate me. There was a look of pure joy in her watery eyes.

"Wade would have been so proud of you—your father too," she said.

I knew that Wade was with me in spirit. I was looking forward to visiting my dad at the VA hospital to tell him about the game.

Vernon Shields was next to recognize Jefferson's achievement. He invited me to participate in an upcoming basketball clinic at the rec center. "Perhaps you can demonstrate that pass you made, maybe tell the young players never to try it in a big game."

Chett Biffmann appeared next, saying he had heard through channels that I had mothballed Wade's truck in the carport at my apartment.

"That true?"

"Yes, sir, but I think Wade's truck will be safe there."

"First of all, buddy boy, it's not Wade's truck any longer. It's yours."

"Yes, sir." I had avoided accepting that responsibility, but I knew Chett was right. It was time to take ownership.

"You've got to think about weather conditions with that antique. I've been holding space 1046 for just the right customer. I can make you one helluva deal, if you're interested."

I was. And since I was generating income from my part-time job at Chip's, I knew I could afford it. Chett had been a friend to Wade over the years, and I appreciated his extending the courtesy.

"You'll need to speak with Nathan about working extra hours to pay those inflated monthly rates at Biffmann Self-Storage."

That was Chip Spears, offering up a good-natured verbal poke to Chett's ribcage. I knew that Chip and Chett talked often as independent business leaders and friends. Chett's chin jostled against his thick neck as he moseyed away to allow me a moment of private time with my boss.

I expressed my gratitude to Chip for his kindness in arranging for Jefferson's fourteenth uniform.

"The store tries to go the extra mile for its employees," Chip said. "I would have extended the same courtesy to Nathan if the college had fallen short of chessboards for the state tournament."

Nathan must have heard Chip say his name. He descended the stands and extended his hand. "No excessive celebrating tonight, rookie. Your shift starts tomorrow at nine a.m."

When I asked Nathan if he had seen Lawrence, Nathan pointed up to the cheap seats.

72

Sometimes Much Can Be Learned from a Goal Not Achieved

I squinted and focused on Lawrence. He was looking everywhere but down at me. I hiked to the top of the arena.

When I arrived, Lawrence threw up his hand to silence me
while he angled his head above the seven No. 2 pencils ar-
rayed in a heptagonal configuration on the bench in front of
him.

He reached for his pad and scribbled a note.

*The 7th Dimension wanted me to remind
you that we are the air inside the ball, we're
part of something bigger, and we must*

remember that everyone is on their own evolutionary path.

"What does it mean?"

Lawrence set down his pad and pencil and leaned in close. "It means you and I can't tell anyone what happened between you and Wade," he whispered. "The Entity says people need to find out for themselves."

That was good enough for me. No one would believe my story anyway.

I was making my way back down the stairs when Lawrence surprised me by shouting my name, his voice cutting through the buzz in the arena. "Hey, Zeke!"

I turned around. "What?"

Lawrence's eyes met mine. He was pointing the front part of his fist at me. "Pound it, bro!" he said.

I jogged back up the steps and landed a fist bump. Immediately after contact, Lawrence sprung open the palm of his hand in a symbolic finger explosion and howled in laughter. The euphoric moment was as much mine as his.

On my way down, I saw a woman waving at me who was the spitting image of Mrs. Fenner.

"Cheese and crackers, Zeke!" Sighting confirmed. "Curfew tonight is ten p.m. Make a good decision."

When I stepped back onto the court, Coach Kincaid left the media scrum to join me.

"Good decision-making was in strong supply today," Coach said. "I thought you made the right call when you dished that ball off to Brock."

Coach and I spent time breaking down the game and evaluating our team's performance. He was curious about my thoughts on Curtis's recovery and Stretch's ability to balance his studies with painting and basketball.

Darla Davenport left the media area and arrived as Coach Kincaid asked his final question. "That no-look wraparound bounce pass to Brock—it's been a long while since I've seen a player pull that off in competition. Have you been working on it long?"

"That was the first time I've ever tried it."

Darla flipped open her reporter's notebook and wrote down my words. "Looks like I've got my lede," she said.

"Anything else?" I asked as the guys celebrated our victory with students, family, and friends.

"Yeah, it seemed like you might have hesitated on that fast break, just before you made the pass to Brock. Care to comment?"

I told Darla that I always worked to get to a position where I could explore all options and choose the right path to success.

"I'll take that as a yes."

I looked beyond where Darla was standing and couldn't believe my eyes. Making his way directly toward me was KU head coach Bob Worth. He stood behind Darla and listened in on the rest of our interview.

"Were you worried about whether Brock would hit that shot, that maybe you should have taken it yourself?"

Darla had come a long way as a sports reporter for the

Jefferson Journal that semester. That was one of the best questions anyone has ever asked me, before or since.

"Sometimes much can be learned from a goal not achieved," I said.

Darla darted out of the gym to file her story. That left Bob Worth and me standing face-to-face. I extended my hand to the legendary basketball coach.

"I see you've been practicing that," Bob Worth said. "It's the grip of a confident leader. I see why Coach Kincaid had you running point on that last play."

By then, my handshake was as second nature as hitting the open man.

Coach Worth was a long way from eastern Kansas. I wondered what he was doing in Los Angeles. I didn't have to wait long to find out.

"I'm in town with my staff to scout some young fellas from Westside. Imagine my surprise when you checked into the game. I'd heard you left the team."

It was no secret that Bob Worth had good sources of intel in basketball circles, even at the community college level on the West Coast.

"I was dealing with some family issues. Coach Kincaid allowed me to rejoin the team when I resolved them."

A couple of Coach Worth's staff members circled over to tell him it was time to go, so I knew my time with him would be cut short.

"What are your plans for your junior year, son?"

"No plans yet, Coach."

"My original offer still stands. No promises, just an opportunity to come to the birthplace of basketball to prove yourself, in the classroom and on the court."

I thanked Bob Worth for his kind offer and promised to let him know. Then I went to the bench and gathered my gear. I was about to stand up when I heard a familiar voice from behind.

"Kansas, huh? Not sure that state's big enough for both of us."

It was Rebecca.

The day's roller-coaster ride hadn't been insane enough. To cap it off, my former girlfriend had walked into the gym. Rebecca's hair was shorter, and she was wearing a blue windbreaker with the Jayhawks mascot on it.

She leaned in and kissed me.

"Good thing Brock bailed you out, champ."

I let that go. "What are you doing here?"

"I needed to come back for the rest of my things. When Brock called to tell me about the game, I bought my bus ticket to arrive a week early."

That was a new indoor record for Brock. He had done two things right in the same calendar month.

I had thought I would never see Rebecca again, but there we were, hanging out together in the afterglow of the championship.

"How's it going?" I asked.

"Better. Been doing a lot of journaling, making new friends, finding some peace. It's really good to see you again."

After the brief awards ceremony, Rebecca and I talked for a while about her semester at the University of Kansas. She filled me in on her classes in KU's Department of Health, Sport, and Exercise Sciences and her experiences working as a volunteer with the athletics department.

"You should go be with your friends," she said.

"Truth is, I'd rather be spending my time with you."

"How about you drive me home in that ancient relic you call a truck?"

I explained to Rebecca why I had opted instead for my bike as we made our way to the exit.

There were a lot of things weighing on me as we were leaving, starting with my dad's health. I planned to visit him the next day to tell him that we had won the championship. I was hoping the news would spark the beginning of his recovery.

I needed to get to the bottom of my otherworldly encounter with Wade. There was so much weird information to process that I barely knew where to start.

Then there was the matter of the 7th Dimension's suspension of my nomination for a basketball guardianship. I had no idea if I would ever get a second chance.

But in that moment, as I stood next to Rebecca and waved goodbye to Curtis and Stretch, I knew everything would be okay.

Rebecca and I left the gym, and I walked her home, just like old times.

ACKNOWLEDGMENTS

The list of people who were instrumental in the creation of this novel once again starts with my editor, Judy Gitenstein, whose deep knowledge of the art and science of storytelling helped make this book possible.

Christopher Caines returned as my copyeditor, ensuring the fitness and accuracy of my words. His sense of humor and extensive knowledge of basketball were an added bonus.

Marco Pavia, my kind and generous book producer, returned to handle design and production chores. He may well be the most level-headed creative person I know.

Tabitha Lahr (cover designer), Brent Wilcox (interior page designer), and Sara Dyck, Cecile Garcia, and Kammy Wood (proofreaders) came back to apply their considerable talents.

I am blessed to have such an awesome group of dedicated beta readers, namely Hailey Star Dowthwaite, Sam Hertzog, Santos Rodriguez, Megan Walker, and Drew Weschler.

U.S. Marine Corps Staff Sergeant Joshua J. Cullins of the 1st Explosive Ordnance Disposal Company, 1st Marine Logistics Group, I Marine Expeditionary Force from Camp Pendleton, California, died on October 19, 2010, while conducting combat operations in Helmand province, Afghanistan, during Operation Enduring Freedom. Staff Sergeant Cullins served as the model for Wade Archer, older brother of Zeke, the book's protagonist.

U.S. Marine Corps Captain and Executive Officer Juan F. Rodriguez of the 1st Explosive Ordnance Disposal Company—whom I met at a street dedication in Los Angeles for Staff Sergeant Cullins—lent his expertise as my military advisor.

I had the good fortune to spend time with Fr. Robert W. Hale, O.S.B. Cam., of the New Camaldoli Hermitage in Big Sur, California, to discuss the merits and challenges of leading a righteous life. Fr. Robert's wisdom can be found throughout these pages.

Bob Conroy, engineering faculty member emeritus from Cal Poly San Luis Obispo, returned to assist with the mathematical and scientific aspects of the book.

Roger J. Couture, author of *Surfing with Snakes & Dragons*, served as my trusted surfing advisor.

Chef Wills Carter and Katherine A. Bloxsom-Carter, the proprietors of The Canyon Villa in Paso Robles, California, shared their take on the ethereal art of breadmaking, which led to the recipe for Nathan Freeman's grandmother's baked-bread chess pieces.

I read a series of books that helped to shape my creation of the inter-dimensional energy being I named the 7th Dimension. The list includes *A Brief History of Time* by Stephen Hawking, *Life After Death* and *Unseen Forces* by Dr. Robert Davis, *An End to Upside Down Thinking* by Mark Gober, *Wholeness and the Implicate Order* by David Bohm, *Synchronized Universe: New Science of the Paranormal* by Claude

Swanson, *Cosmos* by Carl Sagan, and *Fearless Intelligence* by Michael Benner.

Curtis Marsh, KU Endowment Associate Development Director, provided behind-the-scenes access to Allen Fieldhouse as well as encouragement and historical insight into the University of Kansas basketball program.

Brian Minkoff lent his knowledge of regional sub-dialects of the English Midlands. Nathan Jones offered assistance with the Welsh language.

Jon Haim of Mount Sinai Memorial Parks and Mortuaries in Los Angeles assisted with Wade Archer's funeral service particulars.

I'm grateful to the numerous book clubs across the country that have taken the time to read and comment on *This Was Never About Basketball* (aka book one), and I'm hoping they will take on this one as well. In particular, I would like to acknowledge Cheryl Sparks and the SeaSpects Bookclub, Jillian Ann Mack and the Bella Book Club, and Martha Russell and the TLC Ladies of Arcadia.

I've already offered Samuel Adam "Shmuli" Weber the role of Sherman "Lawrence" Tuckerman when this book series is made into a feature film.

My friends Steve and Ann Hertzog provided ground support in Lawrence, Kansas, and opened many doors for me there.

My book publicist, the venerable Irwin Zucker, deserves a special mention here for his tireless efforts in securing countless radio interviews for me.

Sally Bookbinder's frank and honest feedback on book one helped to keep me on the path as I pounded out this next installment.

I have a group of friends who provided ongoing encouragement and support during the creation of this book. The lineup includes Lilly Akpobome, Rob Anker, Judy Davidson, Ted Dayton, Jasmine Ilkhan, Larry Jonas, Neal Laybhen, Stanley Malone, Jill Moreno, Mason Nesbitt, Cary Osborne, Tim Riley, Kip "Chip Spears" Sears, Jane Stanton, James Stewart, Shirley Strickland, Trevor Thompson, Rich Veum, John Walker, Steve Waugh, Angela Weber, and Bobbie Yunis.

I'd also like to mention two intangibles that have helped to open hidden passageways within. One is coffee from the Yirgacheffe micro-region of southern Ethiopia. The other is my secret stash of Snow Lion Tibetan incense, which contains fifty-five ingredients (allegedly including cow dung) and is purportedly hand-rolled by Nepalese monks.

Early in the creation of this book, I had a graveside conversation at Eden Memorial Park Cemetery in Mission Hills, California, with my father, Jack Leener, who was no doubt communicating with me directly from his lofty perch in the hereafter. That experience led to the concept of untethered human consciousness as a central story point. Thanks, Dad—way to come up big.

The creative support from my son, Zachary, and his wife, Erika, had an immeasurable impact on this work.

My wife, Andrea, believed in me, even when the words went on an extended sabbatical in the early going.

ABOUT THE AUTHOR

Craig Leener grew up on the basketball courts of the San Fernando Valley in Los Angeles, California.

He has studied the game as a player, coach, referee, fan, and sportswriter.

Craig earned an associate degree in liberal arts from Los Angeles Valley College and a bachelor's degree in radio, TV, and film from California State University, Northridge.

He worked within the entertainment industry in film operations, post-production technical services, and human resources management before finding his calling as a sportswriter and young adult novelist.

Craig sits on the board of directors of the Journalism Alumni Association at CSUN, where he mentors student journalists and serves as the organization's director of scholarships.

Craig is a member of the North Valley Family YMCA and lives in the suburbs of Los Angeles with his wife, Andrea.

Made in the USA
San Bernardino, CA
11 September 2019